Leo

A Sign of Love Novel

Mia Sheridan

Copyright © 2013 Mia Sheridan

All rights reserved, including the right to reproduce, distribute, or transmit in any form or by any means.

ISBN-10: 1490339973
ISBN-13: 978-1490339979

COVER ARTIST: MIA SHERIDAN
FORMATTED BY MIDNIGHT ENGEL PRESS

This book is a work of fiction. Names, characters, places, and incidents are the product of the author's imagination or are used fictitiously. Any resemblance to actual events, locales, or persons, living or dead, is coincidental.

This book is dedicated to my husband.
You are the true-life inspiration for every fictional hero
my mind and my heart dream up.

The Leo

A passionate lover by nature and a brave fighter by instinct.

CHAPTER ONE

Evie is Fourteen, Leo is Fifteen

I'm sitting on the roof outside my bedroom window, staring up at the dark night's sky, watching my breath plume in the cold November air. I pull the ratty, pink blanket more tightly around myself and rest my head on my knees, tucked tightly to my chest. Suddenly, a small stone lands on the roof next to me and then slides back down the slight incline to the ground. I lift my head and grin as I hear him begin the climb up the ramshackle trellis on the side of the house. One more pound and that dilapidated thing won't hold him. That doesn't matter anymore though. He won't be here to climb it. My heart squeezes painfully at the thought, but I school my expression as he makes it over the ledge and crawls toward me, all gangly limbs and shaggy, dark-blond hair. He smiles warmly as he sits up next to me, showing me that small gap between his front teeth that I love so much. I sway toward him, and we sit forehead to forehead for several minutes, staring into each other's eyes before he sighs and sits up straight.

"I don't think I'm going to survive without you, Evie," he says, sounding like he's holding back tears.

I bump my shoulder on his. "That's a little dramatic, don't you think, Leo?" I say, trying to tease a smile out of him. It works.

But then the smile disappears and he scrubs a hand down his face. He pauses for a minute and then says, "No. It's a fact."

I don't know what to say. How can I comfort him when I feel the exact same way?

He looks over at me again and we stare into each other's eyes once more.

"Why are you looking at me?" I ask, using a line I know he'll understand. It was the first thing I ever said to him.

His expression doesn't change for a minute, and then a slow smile spreads over his face. "Because I like your face," he says, grinning now, showing me that gap again and delivering his own line perfectly. He's skinny and scrappy and shaggy haired, and he's the most beautiful boy I've ever seen. I don't ever want to stop looking at him. I don't ever want to stop being near him. But he's moving across the country, and there's nothing we can do. We met in the first foster care home we each were sent to. He's my best friend in the world, the boy I've grown to love intensely, the boy who's finally made it safe to dream. But he's been adopted. I'm so happy for him to finally have a family, because it's so rare for that to happen to teens. But at the same time, my heart feels like it's bleeding inside my chest.

He's looking at me intensely now like he can read my mind. Which of course, he can. Maybe I'm an open book, or maybe love is like a magnifying glass straight into the souls of those who own your heart.

He keeps looking at me silently for several seconds, and then I can tell by his expression that he's made a decision. Before I can wonder what that is, he leans toward me and brushes his lips softly across mine. Tiny sparks seem to ignite in the air around us, and I shiver slightly. He scoots closer to me and holds my face in his hands. He looks straight into my eyes, his lips still inches from my own and whispers, "I'm going to kiss you now, Evie, and when I do, it's going to mean that you're mine. I don't care how far away from each other we are. You. Are. Mine. I'll wait for you. And I want you to wait for me. Promise me you won't let anyone else touch you. Promise me you'll save yourself for me, and only me."

The whole world has stopped and it's just us, sitting here on a roof in the middle of a November night. "Yes," I whisper back, the word *reverberating through my mind. Yes, yes, yes, a million times, yes.*

He pauses, still staring into my eyes, and I want to scream at him, "Kiss me already!" My body is heady with anticipation.

And then his lips are on mine again, and THIS is a kiss. It starts out gentle, his soft lips nibbling at mine tenderly. But then something inside him shifts, and suddenly he's running his tongue along the seam of my lips, asking for entrance. A thrill races down my spine as I open to him, letting out an involuntary moan, and hearing me, he moans back. His tongue flirts with mine—caressing, gently dueling—and I feel like my body is going to implode with pleasure at the taste of him. We fumble along for a few minutes, and even our inexperience is delicious in its exploration. Or at least I think so, and I hope he does, too. We're learning and memorizing each other's mouths. Before long, we're like two dance partners, moving in perfect synchronicity, living out a passionate choreography of lips and tongues.

I lay back on the roof, holding him to me as we continue kissing. We kiss for hours, days, weeks, a lifetime perhaps. Our kiss is blissful oblivion. It's too much and not nearly enough.

It's my first kiss and I know it's his, too. And it is perfection.

Suddenly, I feel something wet and cold hitting my cheeks, and it brings me back to the here and now. I open my eyes and he does, too, as we both realize big, fluffy snowflakes are falling down around us. We both laugh with wonder. It's as if the angels arranged this show just for us, making the most memorable moment of our lives that much more magical.

He rolls off me and I'm immediately freezing. I know I need to get inside and he needs to go back home. The realization washes over me and a lump forms in my throat. Tears begin rolling down my cheeks.

He pulls me to him, and we cling to each other for long moments, gathering the strength to say goodbye.

He pulls back and the look of torment on his face is heartbreaking. "This is not goodbye, Evie. Remember our promise. Don't ever forget our promise. I will come back for you. I'll write to you with my new address *as soon as I get to San Diego and we'll stay in touch that way. I want to be able to carry your letters with me and re-read them again and again. I'll send you my phone number, too, just in case, but I want you to write to me, okay? Then before we know it, you'll be eighteen, and I'll be able to come back for you. We'll make a life together."*

"Okay," I whisper. "Write to me as soon as you get there, okay?"

"I will. It's the first thing I'll do." He pulls me against him one last time and kisses the tears off my cheeks. Then he turns and makes his way to the trellis. As he begins the descent, he looks back at me and says quietly, "It will only ever be you, Evie."

It's the last thing he ever says to me. I never see Leo again.

CHAPTER TWO

Eight Years Later

Someone is following me. He's been doing it for a week and a half now. He's crap at it. I marked him almost immediately and I've been watching him as he's been watching me. Clearly, he's no professional. But I can't think of one single reason why someone is following me around town. Especially someone who looks like this guy. I've heard that one of the reasons many serial killers are successful at luring victims is because they look like nice, good-looking, average guys. But I still can't believe that the Adonis trailing me is someone to worry too much about, safety wise. Maybe I'm being naïve, but it's just a gut feeling. My upbringing trained me to recognize a threat immediately, and I'm just not feeling one from him. Plus, he's more the type that you *ask*—maybe even beg—to pull you into a dark alleyway, than the one you mace for doing so. I've stared at him with a strategically placed compact, through a slat in my blinds, and via the reflection in store windows so easily, I'm almost embarrassed at his laughable stalking skills. Clearly, he wouldn't be an asset to any ninja organization anywhere, ever.

But the question remains, what does he want? I have to believe it's some kind of case of mistaken identity. Perhaps he's a really inept P.I. who has latched onto the wrong girl for one of his clients.

He's not trailing me today, though, which is good because I'm going to a funeral, and I'd prefer not to deal with the distraction. Willow is being buried today. Beautiful Willow, named after the tree with the long branches, made to sway and bend in the wind. Only Willow hadn't bent when the cold wind blew. She broke. She shattered. She said she'd had enough and stuck a needle in her arm. A breath hitches in my throat as I picture her pretty face, always tainted by the sad, wary expression.

We grew up together in foster care and neither one of our lives had started out as much of a fairy tale. I met her in the first house I was sent to, after a neighbor called the police because of a loud party my birth mom was having. When the police showed up, I was sitting on the couch in my pink Care Bears pajamas, a guy who smelled like tooth decay and beer had his hand up my nightgown, too wasted to move away from me quickly enough, and there were several baggies of meth on the coffee table. My birth mom sat on the couch across from me, watching disinterestedly. I don't know if she just didn't care, or was too wasted to care. I guess in the end, it doesn't really matter.

I sat unmoving as the police hauled the guy off me. I had learned by that point that fighting was pointless. Disappearing was my best option, and if I couldn't do it in a closet or under a bed, I would disappear into my own head. I was ten.

I thought of that first foster home like a junk drawer. You know, the one you keep in your kitchen for all the little odds and ends you don't know what else to do with, that have no home? We were all the random pieces tossed there, no relationship to anything else, save for the fact we were all *miscellaneous*.

A couple days after I arrived, Willow showed up, a pretty little blonde pixie with haunted eyes. She didn't talk much, but that first night, she climbed into my bed, settled herself between the wall and me and curled up into a little ball. She whimpered in her sleep and begged someone to stop hurting her. I didn't have to wonder too hard about what had happened to her.

I watched out for her as much as I could after that, even though she was only a year younger than I. Neither one of us was exactly a force to be reckoned with—two broken little girls who had already learned that trusting people was a risky business—but Willow seemed even more fragile than me, like the smallest hurt would cause her to crumble. So I took the blame and the punishment for things that were her fault. I let her sleep with me every night, telling her stories to try and soothe the demons away. I didn't have a lot of gifts in this world, but I was good at telling stories, and I wove tales together for her in an effort to make sense of her nightmares. Truth be told, they were as much for me as they were for her. I was trying to understand, too.

Through the years, I did what I could to love that girl. Lord knows I did. But as much as I wanted to and as hard as I tried, I couldn't *save* Willow. I didn't think anyone could have because the sad fact was, Willow didn't want to be saved. Early on, Willow had been taught that she was unlovable, and she wove that lie into her soul until it was what she lived and breathed. It was the basis for every choice she made, and for every heart she broke, including mine.

A month after Willow and I'd moved in, an eleven-year-old boy showed up in our house, a tall, skinny, angry kid named Leo who grunted yes and no answers to our foster parents and barely looked anyone in the eye. When he got there, he had one arm in a cast, and fading, yellowish bruises on his face, and what looked like finger marks on his neck. It seemed like he was angry at the world and common sense told me he had good reason for that sentiment.

Leo . . . Leo. But I know I can't think of him. I don't let my mind go there because it's too painful. Of all the things I've lived through, he is the one thing I can't bear to dwell on for very long. He has a place in my past and that's where I leave him . . . as much as my mind and my heart are able.

I snap out of my reverie as the minister signals me to the front for the eulogy. Unfortunately, Willow had never made friends with people who roll out of their own pit of despair as early as nine o'clock on a Sunday morning, so my audience is small, and at least half of them look like they're hung-over, if not still drunk. I stand behind the podium and face the group, and that's when I see him, leaning against a tree several feet back from the rest of the gathering. The sight of him here startles me. I was sure I wasn't being followed. But how and why would he be here if he hadn't trailed me? I know for a fact I had never seen him with Willow. I would have remembered this guy. I stare at my mystery stalker for a moment, and he keeps eye contact, an unreadable expression on his face. It's the first time our eyes have met. I shake my head slightly to bring myself back to the moment and begin speaking.

"Once upon a time a very special, beautiful little girl was sent to a faraway land by the angels to live an enchanted life, full of love and happiness. They called her The Glass Princess because her laugh reminded them of the tinkling, glass bells that were hung on heaven's gate and would chime each time a new soul was welcomed. But her name was also appropriate for her because she was very sensitive and loved very deeply, and hers was a heart that could be easily broken.

"During the arrangement of her trip to this faraway land, one of the newer angels made a mistake, and a mix up occurred, sending The Glass Princess to a place she wasn't supposed to be - a dark, ugly area, ruled mostly by gargoyles and other evil creatures. But when a soul is placed in human skin, it is a permanent situation that cannot be changed. Although the angels cried in anguish for the fate The Glass Princess would have to bear, there was nothing they could do, other than to watch over her and try their best to lead her in the right direction, away from the land of gargoyles and evil creatures.

"Unfortunately, very soon after The Glass Princess arrived in this land, the cruelty of the beasts around her created the first large crack in her very breakable heart. And although many other less evil creatures tried to love and care for the princess—for she was very beautiful and very easy to love—the princess's heart continued to crack until it crumbled completely, leaving the princess heartbroken forever.

"The princess closed her eyes for the last time, thinking of all the evil monsters who had been cruel to her and caused her heart to shatter. But evil creatures, no matter how demented they are, never get the last word. The angels, always nearby, swooped down and carried The Glass

Princess back up to heaven where they put her broken heart back together, never to be hurt again. The princess opened her eyes and smiled her beautiful smile and laughed her beautiful laugh. And it still sounded like the tinkling glass bells, just as it always had. The Glass Princess was home at last."

I make my way back through the group, some faces slack, some slightly confused. I'm sure they wonder why I just told a children's fairy tale at a funeral for a drug addict. But that's between Willow and me, and somewhere, I feel sure she heard it and is smiling. I glance at the man leaning against the tree and he seems frozen, his eyes still fixed on mine. I frown slightly. If I knew Willow, his presence probably isn't anything positive. God, did she owe money to someone? Has he been following me to figure out if I'm someone he can collect from on her behalf? I frown again. Surely not. I think it's pretty clear after about thirty seconds, that my financial portfolio is, um, *lacking*.

"I don't know exactly what that meant, honey, but it was pretty," Sherry, Willow's roommate—and by roommate, I really mean that that's where Willow crashed when she wasn't mooching off some boyfriend—says, smiling, pulling me aside and giving me a quick hug.

Sherry's a little rough and looks about ten years older than she actually is. Her hair is dyed blonde, with about an inch of dark roots mixed liberally with gray. She's baring way too much cleavage for a funeral, or for that matter, cage dancing. Her skin is leathery and overly tanned, and she's wearing a thick layer of makeup. Her platform, stripper shoes round out the look. But despite the myriad of fashion faux pas, she's a good-hearted person and tried her damndest to be a friend to Willow. She learned the same lesson I had learned though—if someone is hell-bent on self-destruction, there isn't a lot you can do to change their mind.

When I look again, mystery man is gone.

CHAPTER THREE

I bussed it to the cemetery, but Sherry gives me a ride back to my apartment, calling out, "Keep in touch, honey!" as I dash from her car, thanking her and waving goodbye.

I rush inside and quickly change out of my sleeveless black dress and heels and pull on the uniform I wear for my day job. I'm a hotel housekeeper at the Hilton during the day and work part-time for a catering company as a server, mostly on weekend evenings, or when I'm called. It's not glamorous, but I do what I have to do to pay the rent. I take care of myself and I'm proud that I do. I knew the day I turned eighteen, I'd be shown the door of the foster home I was living in, which both thrilled and scared me to death. I was finally free of being a part of the system, free to make my own rules and my own destiny, but I was also more alone than I had ever been in my life. No family and no safety net to land on, not even guaranteed a roof over my head or three meals a day anymore. I had to talk myself through my share of panic attacks. But four years later and I'm doing just fine. I mean, depending on what your definition of just fine is? I guess it's a relative question.

It's not that I don't want more for myself. I know that I tend to "play it safe" when it comes to most things, including ambition. But I also figure I started out with enough drama and heartache to last a lifetime and "safe" might be boring, but it's also something that's coveted by someone who never had it. And so for now, I'm content.

After hopping off the bus downtown, I walk quickly to the employee entrance of the large hotel and clock in just in time. I stock a housecleaning cart and make my way to the top of the hotel, beginning on the floor where the penthouse is located. I knock quietly and when there's no response, I open the door with my passkey. I wheel the cart in and take in the room. It seems vacated if not slightly trashed, and so I begin stripping the bed. I turn up my iPod and sing along to Rihanna. I smile and shake my ass as I put a fresh sheet on the king-sized bed. This is one thing I do love about this job. I can get lost in my own head, the cleaning a monotonous background activity. I pull the fresh duvet up on the bed and begin turning it down when I catch movement out of the corner of my eye and whirl around, jumping slightly and letting out a choked sound of surprise. There's a man standing behind me, a smirk on his face, leaning casually in the doorway of the bedroom. I take my ear buds out and blink rapidly, embarrassed. "I'm so sorry," I say. "I didn't think anyone was here. If you need me to return later, I'll be happy to do that." I smooth my hands down the skirt of my dress nervously. His eyes follow my hands and continue down my legs before moving slowly back to my eyes. My heartbeat picks up in speed, anxiety coursing through my body.

I start moving my cart toward the doorway. He advances rapidly, startling me, and grabbing on to the handle of my cart. "Really, it's fine," he says, his voice smooth. "We were just leaving. I was just enjoying the show." He grins, and his eyes lazily run up my body again, from my feet to my breasts, and I fidget uncomfortably. That's when a woman walks in to the room. She's beautiful, her blonde hair perfectly coiffed, her makeup flawless, and I feel immediately self-conscious. I nod my head in her direction and begin moving toward the door. "I'll come back," I murmur, but both of them are moving toward the door as well and as they do, the woman says, "Really, we're just leaving. Stay and finish up." She offers me a look of disdain as she shrugs on her jacket, and says, "And make sure you empty the trash. The last girl who was in here forgot to do that." The man smiles toward her and pats her on the ass as she's scooting out the door, and she lets out a giggle.

I stand motionless for a minute after the door has shut behind them, trying to recoup the careless attitude I had before they interrupted me. But my mood has suddenly shifted and I feel melancholy in a way I don't really want to think about.

I finish up my shift, and as I clock out, my friend Nicole rushes up behind me and swipes her time card.

"Damn slobs on the twelfth floor," she rants. "I swear, you'd think some of the people who stay here were raised in a barn. It took me two hours to clean three rooms on that floor. Disgusting. Don't even ask. Now I'm late to pick up Kaylee. Walk with me to the bus stop? My car is in the shop." She grabs for her coat as she's talking.

I grin at her and shrug on my own coat as we walk toward the door. "Maybe we could make up a 'for the consideration of your housecleaning crew' list to hand out at check in?" I offer sarcastically.

"Yes! Number one, please for the love of *God*, wrap your used condoms in toilet paper and deposit them in the trash. It is beyond my job description to scrape your dried . . . *stuff* off the carpet after you toss the thing under the bed."

I fake a vomiting noise, but I'm laughing as we hurry toward the bus stop. "Okay," I continue, "number two, please don't clip your toenails in bed. I prefer not to get a clippings shower when I shake out your comforter and then have to go around on my hands and knees attempting to collect them all off the floor."

"Oh God! Truly? Animals!" But she's laughing, too, as she shakes her blonde head.

Her bus is just pulling up to her stop so I give her a quick hug goodbye saying, "See you Wednesday night," as I start walking across the street to my stop going in the other direction.

Nicole never ceases to make me smile with her carefree attitude and funny sense of humor. She's married to a really great guy named Mike and they have a four-year-old daughter, Kaylee. Mike is an electrician and makes good money, but Nicole works housekeeping a couple days a week to bring in a little extra and as she says, to enhance her shoe budget. She's got a thing for shoes, the higher the better. I don't know how she walks in some of those things.

Nicole and I hit it off quickly when I met her at work three years ago. She and Mike have me over for dinner at least once a week. I love spending time with them and Kaylee, soaking in the joy and comfort that is a loving family, doing nothing more special than having a meal together and sharing their evening. What they don't fully get is that, to me, a loving family dinner isn't just special, it's everything. Everything I never had.

Nicole and Mike know that I grew up in foster care, but not too much beyond that. They're kind, hardworking people who live in a cute two-bedroom house in a decent neighborhood, and I don't want to bring stories of drug abuse, pimps, and molestation into their world. Not that they're naïve about the fact that all of that stuff goes on, but in a lot of ways, they're my bubble, my safe place away from that world, and I want to keep it that way.

I pull out my novel and start reading as the bus begins its journey across town to my apartment. I'm so engrossed I almost miss my stop, jumping up just in time to make it through the closing door. I walk the five blocks to my apartment and let myself in through the front door, shaking my head at the broken, *again*, lock. Okay, so security isn't exactly high, but it's decently clean, and it has a sunny balcony off the back where I can grow a few fruit trees in containers and several pots of flowers. Sometimes I sit out there in the evenings with a good book, feeling content. And it's enough.

I'm slightly disappointed that my stalker is obviously off duty this evening. It's not lost on me that this is not the healthiest of thoughts. I smile anyway.

I take a shower, standing under the spray longer than I know I should. Hot water doesn't come for free. But I allow myself this little luxury today as I shed the tears I knew would come for Willow. "Rest in peace, princess," I whisper as the warm spray washes over me, mixing with my tears. After not too long, I get out and towel off.

I pull on a pair of yoga pants, and a sweatshirt that falls off my shoulders and trudge into the kitchen to make myself some dinner. I heat up some of the homemade vegetable soup I made a couple days ago, and toast some bread. There's enough soup left to put in a small Tupperware container, so I ladle it in and then walk down the hall to Mrs. Jenner's apartment, knocking lightly. When she answers, I smile and say, "Have you eaten yet? I have some homemade veggie soup if you haven't." I know Mrs. Jenner is on a very fixed income since her husband died and so if I ever have anything extra, I bring it to her.

She smiles brightly and says, "Oh dear, you're always so sweet. Thank you so much."

I smile back, saying, "You're welcome. Night, Mrs. Jenner."

Back in my kitchen, I put my own dinner on a tray and take it back into the only other small room. I sit on the floor and lean against my loveseat as I eat. A studio apartment doesn't allow for a lot of furniture, but that's okay because it's not like I entertain. I put *The Shawshank Redemption*, one of my favorite movies, into the DVD player and push play. I don't spend the extra money on cable, so I rely on the DVDs I've picked up at garage sales. I'd usually rather read anyway, so it's fine by me.

After I clean up my dishes, I end up falling asleep in front of the movie and when I finally drag myself into bed, it's after midnight.

****

My alarm goes off at seven, and I pull myself out of bed and put on my running gear. It's a chilly morning and so I pull on earmuffs and a fleece jacket. I take a minute or two to stretch outside my apartment, my breath coming out in white puffs in front of me as I take off down the street. I tighten my fist around the door key I have in my pocket, like the self-defense instructor taught us to do in the course I took at the community college. It gives me comfort. I hold onto it until I jog into the semi-populated running track of the park, and then I zip my pocket closed with the key inside and take out my earbuds and push play on my iPod. I run my usual three miles and return home, feeling strong and energized.

    I take a quick shower and dry my long, dark hair. After putting it up into a ponytail, I pull on a pair of worn jeans and an oversized gray sweater. It's my day off, and I'm going to do nothing more than putter around, make a trip to the library, and spend the rest of the day on my balcony under a blanket, with a good book and a cup of tea. I wonder briefly if this plan might qualify me for early social security benefits. While other twenty-two year olds are sleeping in so they're well rested for the club later tonight, I'm taking stock of my tea collection. *Yup.*

    Thirty minutes later, after making my bed and doing a quick pick up of my studio, I'm just beginning the walk down the street to the local neighborhood library, when I spot a dark silver BMW parked about a block up the street from my apartment. I don't know anything about cars, but I note the model on the back, M6. I smile slightly to myself. On duty today, I see.

    I make it to the library and spend about an hour there, picking out a new stack of books for the upcoming week. I have four novels, a budget-friendly cookbook, and a book about The Second World War. I may not have the money right now to go to college, but knowledge is only a library card away, and I pick up a new subject each week.

    As I make my way back to my apartment, I clock tall, dark-ish and handsome about a block behind me, walking leisurely and pretending to talk on his cell phone.

    I make a decision. I pass my own apartment, and I pick up my pace a little, and as I turn the corner, I break into a run and turn into the small alley in the middle of the block. I run down the alley, hoping to double around and come up behind him.

    I'm out of breath as I turn the corner on my own street again and walk very swiftly to the end of the block and peek around the corner. Sure enough, he's standing in the middle of the block, clearly confused and not knowing where I disappeared. I walk quietly up behind him and say loudly, "It's impolite to stalk strangers."

He whirls around and jumps back slightly, as he sucks a loud breath in through his slightly parted mouth. His eyes are wide. "Jesus! You scared the shit out of me!"

"I scared *you*?" I say incredulously, glaring at him. "You're the one following me like a creeper." I cock my head to the side. "By the way, *pointer*, when you're stalking someone, you might want to consider being a little more discreet." I sweep my hand in his direction. "Gawking at your victim in the middle of the street tends to be a giveaway." I narrow my eyes.

He remains silent, staring at me intently, his lips slightly parted. *His lips! They're really nice lips.* Don't be distracted, Evie. He could still be a serial killer! At the very least, a serious *weirdo*.

I put my hands on my hips. "Don't despair though. I'm sure with some study, you could get better. There might be an instructional video or something you could pick up . . . maybe a book on the subject? *Creepy Stalker for Dummies*?" I raise one eyebrow.

He stands still, continuing to stare at me without saying a word for several seconds, and then he bursts out laughing. "Well, holy hell, you really are something, aren't you?" But there's appreciation in his voice. And his laugh. Wow, his laugh is *really* nice.

I study him for a minute. Good God, I thought he was good-looking before. But up close, this man is devastating, all square jaw, straight nose and deep brown eyes. If there is any imperfection to him at all, it's that he's a little *too* perfect, if that's possible. He's tall and broad and very masculine with a shadow of stubble on his jaw that looks more purposeful than unkempt. And when he laughs like that, I swear a piece of my soul—the part of me that keeps secrets even from myself—tries to lunge toward him, like his happiness is an invisible pull to my own heart. It's crazy. I don't even know this guy. And reminder . . . stalker . . . potentially creepy weirdo.

"Okay," I say. "Well, the gig is up. Why are you following me?" I narrow my eyes at him again. But truthfully, I'm not nervous. There are absolutely no danger vibes coming off this guy at all. And I've contended with just about all brands of human fuckery. You could say I'm an *expert* in human fuckery.

Then he does something to knock me off balance completely. He runs his hand through his thick, caramel-brown hair, drops his head so he's looking up at me with his eyes, and raises his eyebrows in a gesture that looks shy and doubtful, yet completely sexy. And I almost swoon. That, right there, that's his deal sealer. I bet that look has girls all over the city dropping their panties right on the spot. I stand up straighter, shocked by my own thoughts. I'm not a swooner. And I'm definitely not a panty dropper.

He speaks and I snap out of it. "I've been that obvious, huh?" And he has the grace to look embarrassed. He takes a step toward me. I take a step back. He stops. "I'm not going to hurt you," he says, sounding like my distrust of him is truly hurtful. I mean, really? Need I remind him again that he's a creepy stalker? And truly, I'm not afraid of him, but I don't know him either, and a healthy distance from strangers is never a bad idea.

"Yes, you've been THAT obvious." I tilt my head and gentle my voice. "Enough games. I want to know why you're following me."

He seems to consider whether to answer me or not. Then he looks me in the eye and says softly, "I knew Leo. He asked me to check on you."

CHAPTER FOUR

My world comes to a screeching halt, and I freeze, my mouth falling open. "What?" I croak out. With one name, he's left me a trembling, reeling mess. I steel myself though. This stranger doesn't need to know that. I straighten up and ask in a stronger voice, "What do you mean you knew Leo?" I don't let on that I'm afraid of what that past tense means.

Of course, I've wondered a thousand times if something happened to Leo, convincing myself that something *had* to have happened to Leo for him not to have contacted me all these years, and especially for him to break his promise to me about writing as soon as he arrived in San Diego. My mind came up with a million scenarios over those first few months about why my beautiful boy disappeared from my world . . . a car wreck on the way from the airport to their new home . . . surprising a robber in their house as they arrived . . . .

When I was sixteen, I went to the library and sorted through California newspapers from the week he moved, in search of any news stories about the untimely demise of a mom, dad and their teenage son. Each fruitless search brought both relief and frustration . . . and more crushing heartbreak.

I even created a fake account on Facebook once and looked up his name, but came up with nothing. I didn't keep an account of my own. There were too many people from my past who might attempt to contact me and *that* I did not need.

The problem was, I had precious little information about Leo's family to go on, except for the fact that his adoptive father worked in a hospital. I didn't know if that meant he was a doctor or an administrator or what, but that piece of information, the city they were moving to, and Leo's name and age is all I ever had to work with.

Of course, my resources were small, a library computer and old newspaper articles, so it's no wonder I never got far.

After my unsuccessful attempts at finding any information on him, I made a vow to myself I would stop wondering all the time. It was too painful, practically unbearable. And so on my eighteenth birthday, the day he had promised to come for me, with tears coursing down my cheeks, I closed my eyes and pictured him smiling at me on a roof under a winter sky, and that's where I left him in my mind.

I look up to see that the man is studying me closely, a small frown on his face, but he doesn't move closer now or attempt to touch me in any way. I turn around and walk to some porch steps a few feet behind me and sit down and take a deep breath. My legs feel shaky. I repeat my question, "What do you mean, you knew Leo?"

He moves slowly toward me and gestures to the other side of the step I'm sitting on, asking silently for permission to sit. I nod. He sits on the other side of the stairs, one step down, turned slightly toward me, and then leans forward, resting his elbows on his muscular thighs. I catch a whiff of his cologne, something clean and woodsy and delicious. He sighs and says, "Leo died in a car accident last year. We were friends, teammates in school. We all thought he might make it for a couple days, but he didn't. We visited him together, and he pulled me aside and told me a little about you. He made me promise to check on you to make sure that you were okay, that you were in a good place, happy. He knew I was moving here to work for my dad's company, and that it would be easy for me to check up on you in person." His brow is furrowed and he's talking slowly, as if he's making sure to deliver the information he's giving me in just the right way. He's also leaving something out. I don't know exactly how I know this, I just do.

I feel numb and confused and I'm silent for several minutes. "I see. What exactly did Leo tell you about me?" I finally ask, glancing down at the man. He's watching me intently.

"Just that he knew you in foster care and you were special to him. He said you lost touch, but he'd always wondered about how your life turned out. That's really all."

I don't say anything and so he continues. "I moved here in June, but it took me a couple months to settle in. Then I finally had the time to dedicate to being the creepster I had promised to be." He smiles at me, looking up through long caramel lashes. But it's a sad smile now. Unsure.

I offer a small smile in return. I will not let on how much his words about Leo hurt. *We lost touch?* And all those years he was alive and well and living in San Diego and never once wrote to me or called or tried in any way to get in touch with me? *Why?* I don't even know how to process the fact that I've just learned he died. That he's *dead.* I need to go home and curl up in a ball for a couple of hours. I need to process this. I stand shakily, and the man jumps to his feet beside me. I wipe my clammy hands on the front of my jeans.

"I'm sorry to hear about Leo," I finally say. "It doesn't sound like you know a lot about our history, but Leo is someone who . . . broke a promise to me. It happened a long time ago, and I don't think about him anymore. There was no reason for him to send you to check on me. If he wanted to know how my life turned out, he should have contacted me himself before . . . well, before.

"All the same, it was nice of you to keep your word to your friend. And now you've done your job. Here I am, fine and dandy. Mission accomplished. Dying wish fulfilled." I force a weak smile, but I'm pretty sure it comes across more as a grimace. He doesn't smile back. He looks pained.

"By the way, who do I have the pleasure of calling my own personal, creepy stalker?"

He does smile then, but it doesn't reach his eyes. "Jake Madsen," he says, still watching my face closely.

"Well, Jake Madsen, a.k.a. creepy stalker, obviously you already know I'm Evelyn Cruise. And you already know to call me Evie." I reach my hand out to shake his and when he grips mine back, it's like tiny sparks pass between our skin, and suddenly all I am is my hand. All the other parts of my body, not being touched by Jake Madsen, have ceased to exist. It's the strangest thing and I wonder if he feels it, too. Judging by the way he's staring intently at our hands, a small smile lifting one side of his lips, he does. Okay, so I guess I have chemistry with this man. Big surprise. Who wouldn't have chemistry with a man who looks like he does? He's probably laughing inside and thinking, *another one? Really?* I'm sure women melt in the streets at his feet daily. It must be very nice for him. And the fact that I'm thinking about melting in the street for a man after I've just heard that the love of my life is no longer of this world, has me really, really confused and not just a little bit weirded out, not to mention hurting. I need to leave.

I'm the first one to pull away and when I do, he frowns and looks up into my eyes.

"'Bye, Jake," I say and turn and walk toward my apartment.

"Evie," he calls, and I turn around. "You're gonna miss me, aren't you?" He's smiling.

"You know, Jake, I think I will." I smile a small smile back and turn around and walk quickly home.

As soon as I close the door behind me, I sink to the floor, roll into the fetal position, and I weep for my beautiful boy, my Leo. My tears are tears of sorrow and loss, confusion and hurt. They are tears for the boy I lost and the boy who threw me away. I've been angry and hurt for so many years, but I find I can still feel grief in knowing that Leo's beautiful soul no longer walks this earth, and the pain in that definitive knowledge is almost too much to bear.

Finally I fall asleep right where I am, but I already know from past experience that you don't have to be awake to cry.

CHAPTER FIVE

Evie is Ten, Leo is Eleven

Dinner in this place is always organized bedlam. My job is to fill the water pitchers and get the glasses for everyone. I stand at the sink filling the second of three tall pitchers while all the other kids move loudly around me, fulfilling their dinner duties. There's talking, laughing, and some fighting amongst the older kids.

I sit down at the table in my usual spot, only this night is different as the new kid, Leo, is sitting sullenly to my left where Alex, a twelve-year-old kid with big ears, used to sit. He left three days ago, off to a more permanent foster home. This place is really just a holding tank for kids who need immediate placement. We'll all end up somewhere different, eventually.

This is Leo's first night here. Leo was in charge of putting the napkins out, and I notice that he put them on the right and they're supposed to go on the left. I only know this because I like to read books like Anne of Green Gables and Little House on the Prairie, and I pick up random things like that from the stories.

As we sit waiting for the food to be set on the table by our foster parents and their two teenage daughters, one of the other foster kids, a thirteen-year-old girl named Allie, with acne and a muffin top that looks painful to me because of the way she accentuates it with the tightest pants she can find, flicks a pea at me from a bowl that's just been set on the table.

"Hey, little whore," she whispers, drawing out the word, and puckering up her lips in a ghastly impression of someone working a kissing booth in hell. "I heard your whore mother didn't show up in court today. She must have been busy sucking someone's dick in an alleyway for pocket change. The apple never falls far off the tree, you know."

My eyes widen, and I feel tears burning the backs of my eyes. I will not cry. I will not cry. I stare down at my plate.

Of course, there are no secrets here in this house. Those who want to can easily enough listen in as the social workers meet with our foster parents in the living room at the front of the house. Then the rumors spread. We're all painfully aware of every nightmare each of us has endured to bring us to this melting pot of despair.

And I know Allie's secrets, too. I know that her mother died and that her father basically lost his mind and couldn't work and couldn't take care of Allie and her sister. But I don't say a word.

I'm holding Willow's hand in mine under the table as she sits to the right of me, and she squeezes my hand gently, her wide eyes staring at her plate.

"I'm just being HONEST, Evie," Allie says, laughing, an ugly snorting sound. "It's better if you face the truth." And why does every deliberately cruel person seem to consider themselves the perfect example of necessary bluntness? As if you're supposed to thank them for mowing over your heart with their special brand of honesty.

I don't answer and Allie quickly finds something of more interest than my silence and me.

After a minute, I look up and the boy named Leo is staring at me. I stare back, but he doesn't look away.

"Why are you looking at me?" I hiss at him, my cheeks turning hot, filled with shame for the exchange he just heard.

He just keeps looking at me for a moment, and then he shrugs. "Because I like your face," he says, but now a corner of his mouth is quirking up in a half smile.

I know he's teasing me, but it doesn't feel mean, and I like the way his words make me feel. I look away, but I'm holding back a smile now, too.

CHAPTER SIX

I wake up the next morning feeling like a Mack truck hit me. I still feel a lump form in my throat when I think of Leo dying in a car accident. I close my eyes and once again, I picture him smiling at me from a roof in wintertime. For the second time in my life, I leave him there in my mind.

I climb into a hot shower, taking all the time I want, not caring in the least about my hot water bill. Today is going to be about comfort. I'm going to laze around, eat ice cream, read, and then head to Nicole and Mike's house for dinner. It's just what I need.

I take time drying my hair until it falls down my back in dark waves and dress in dark, skinny jeans, and a white wraparound sweater that's always made me feel pretty.

I realize I don't have any ice cream in the house and so I decide to head to the store for at least two pints. I'll run an extra mile tomorrow.

As soon as I step out the front door of my building, I see Jake leaning against a car, arms crossed and smiling straight at me. He's wearing a pair of worn-looking jeans and a gray, long-sleeved, thermal shirt over a black T-shirt. This is the first time I've ever seen him wearing jeans; even during the week he followed me around town he was in a suit. It does not escape me that Jake Madsen fills out a pair of jeans *really* well.

I stop and cross my own arms, cocking my head to the right. "Need help 'finding your puppy' I suppose?"

He squints at me with amusement. "I was actually just going to offer you some candy. It's in my van over there." He's grinning now.

Jesus, seriously, is it just me or has he gotten better looking overnight?

I can't help it, I grin back, shaking my head.

I start walking, and he falls in step next to me, and I inhale his clean, woodsy scent. God, he smells good. I open my mouth slightly, wanting to taste his smell in my mouth, too. *Oh my God, did I really just do that?* My cheeks heat. *Please don't let him have seen that!* I don't know what came over me. *Why don't you just lick him now, Evie?* I groan internally.

I turn and look up at his perfect profile. He must be at least six-two. I'm five-five. He's looking straight ahead though. I exhale in relief.

I break the momentary silence. "You know, I'm sure there are girls all over the city who would love the opportunity to be stalked by you. It really doesn't seem fair that you focus all your creepiness on me."

He smiles. "I've decided I like focusing on you though, Evie." He's not smiling anymore. He glances over at me almost nervously, studying me with those soulful brown eyes.

I stop walking and cross my arms over my chest. He stops, too, and I catch him take a quick glance at my breasts, now being plumped up by my arms. *Oh, smooth.* But I like that he looks, I can't help it.

I take a deep breath. "Look, Jake," I say seriously. "You caught me by surprise yesterday, about a person I haven't thought about in a long time, but I'm okay. You don't need to check up on me anymore. My life is fine. It's not exciting. It's not glamorous. But I have everything I need. I'm, um, happy." This last part comes out sounding a little bit more like a question than the statement I meant it to be, but I decide to let that go.

Jake does his hand-through-hair, unsure look, *arrgh! deal sealer!* and says, "I just thought maybe you looked a little upset when you left yesterday. And I did that to you. I just wanted to make sure you were okay *today*, not in general, but today."

He looks so sincere, like he was truly worried about me, that I can't help but smile. "I was fine yesterday," I lie. "I don't like to hear about anyone meeting a tragic end, even someone I don't know anymore. But it's nothing that a little ice cream won't take care of. That's where I'm headed. Want to follow me to the grocery store? One last stalking for old time's sake?" I wink.

He laughs as we start walking again. "I don't think it's stalking if I get an invitation, but yes, I'd love to *accompany* you to the store."

"I don't know if I'm ready for this huge jump in status," I tease. "From stalker to chaperone in a day? You'll think I'm easy."

"Just lead the way, smart-ass," he says, grabbing my hand.

I jolt slightly and look down at our joined hands. *Hand holding?* Okay, this is a little weird. And there's that warm feeling again when our hands touch. Which only serves to further weird me out. *He's just being nice, Evie, because he thinks he's upset you. Get yourself together!* It makes me uncomfortable, though, so I pull my hand away, pretending to search through my purse for my sunglasses. I pop them on even though it's not sunny at all and latch both hands onto my purse strap so he's not tempted to resume the hand holding again.

I steal a glance at him, and he's frowning slightly, but doesn't say anything as we continue walking.

This whole situation is weirder than weird.

"So," I say, to make things less awkward than they've suddenly become, "what does your father's company do?"

He glances quickly at me before answering. "We make a product utilized by the Homeland Security division of the government. Essentially it's an X-ray technology that's used by airports around the world. There are several smaller applications, but that's our main focus."

I nod and he continues, "My father started his company thirty years ago and has a division here and in San Diego, but in recent years, the division here was struggling. I started working with him a couple years ago, and I moved here to get the Cincinnati branch back on solid ground. It was really just a matter of restructuring and replacing some top people who were more interested in lining their own pockets than in the strength of the company."

I nod again as we turn the corner onto the block where the grocery store is. "Your father must trust you a lot to give you responsibility for such a big task so quickly," I say.

He stiffens slightly beside me. "I never gave him much reason to trust me. But he actually passed away almost a year ago, six months before I moved here."

He's frowning again and I don't know what he did to need redemption in his father's eyes, but for some unknown reason, all I want to do is make him smile.

So I grab his hand and hold it between us again as I grin up at him. "I'm just glad you had something to fall back on after the crash and burn of your short-lived creepster career."

He bursts out laughing again, his brown eyes warming, and there's that damn pull. Good grief, my stupid hormones need to relax already.

Things seem to have gotten mighty friendly between Jake and me pretty quickly, and a part of me feels just fine and dandy about this. After all, he's gorgeous, and he seems like a nice guy. But another part of me is a little worried. I really don't know anything about Jake other than the few things he's told me, and his connection to Leo is sending all sorts of confusing messages to my heart, messages I decide not to investigate too much further, at least not now.

I see a beautiful girl with long, red hair walking out of the store as we're walking in. She does a double take as she catches sight of Jake, but he doesn't seem to notice her at all, which makes me smile to myself.

I decide to pick up a few more things than just ice cream since I'm here, and my cart is holding several items when we make it to the ice cream aisle.

"What flavor do you like?" Jake asks, opening the freezer door.

"Butter pecan," I say, opening a freezer door a couple down from where he's standing.

He pulls out a carton of butter pecan at the same time I pull out the same flavor of another brand.

"Why that one?" he asks. "This one is twice the price. It's gotta be the best."

I shake my head. "It's not about price, Jake. This one is the

World's Greatest Ice Cream. Look, it says so right on the carton," I say seriously.

He looks between the two. "Evie," he starts, as if he's explaining something to a five-year-old. "You do know that they can say whatever they want to on the package, right? It doesn't mean it's true."

"Well, see," I counter. "You're right. But you're also wrong. I think that ninety-five percent of knowing you're the greatest is all about confidence. You might *suspect* you're the greatest, you might *hope* you're the greatest, but if you don't have the balls to *proclaim* yourself the greatest in bold packaging, and let your critics test you if they dare, then you probably aren't the greatest. Who can resist the guy who really, truly believes in himself?"

He's staring at me in that intense way again, but I just drop the ice cream in my cart and walk away down the aisle toward the checkout lane, my point made.

When we're finished checking out, Jake pulls out his wallet and tries to pay for my groceries, but I shove his money away and give my own to the clerk, glaring at him until he shakes his head and puts his cash away. Maybe I don't run what sounds like a multi-million dollar company, but I can pay for my own damn groceries.

We make our way back to my apartment, walking in companionable silence, holding two plastic grocery bags each.

"So, can I ask what you meant when you said you didn't give your father much reason to trust you?" I ask, going for casual but hoping he'll clue me in a little bit more about the comments he made earlier. If he's an untrustworthy person, I'd like to know that right up front.

He sighs. "I was a screw up of a kid. I was selfish and messed up, and I did everything my father hoped I wouldn't do. If it was self-destructive, I was first in line. Not exactly any parent's dream."

I give him what I hope is an understanding look, and he glances back at me, sadness in his eyes. It doesn't seem like he expects a response, and so we continue on in silence.

When we get to the front door of my building, I nudge the door open with my foot and pass through.

"There's no lock on the outside door?" Jake asks. When I look back at him, his face is tight and there's a muscle ticking in his jaw. He looks pissed.

"Ah, no. I've called the landlord several times, but clearly, it's not his first priority. It's okay. This is a pretty safe neighborhood. No one's gonna step up and call it *World's Greatest*, but it's decent," I joke, trying to lighten Jake's suddenly tense mood.

Jake follows me, and we walk to my apartment door.

I stop just outside as he sets the bags on the floor and looks at me expectantly. "Um, so, thanks, Jake," I say, no intention of inviting him into my plain, tiny apartment. "It was a way more enjoyable trip than I expected it to be." I smile and continue looking at him, not moving a muscle.

Both of our heads turn as Maurice, my neighbor across the hall, a big, beefy black guy who works construction, opens his apartment door and stands there with his arms crossed, looking suspiciously at Jake. He looks like he could bench a Semi, but he's really a big teddy bear. In exchange for the occasional batch of blueberry muffins (his favorite), or orange cranberry muffins (his second favorite), he looks out for me.

"Hi, Maurice." I grin. "This is Jake. I'm good. It's good, um, we're good," I say, awkwardly.

Maurice continues to look at him as if he recognizes him from a registered sex offender website as Jake takes a few steps and extends his hand, smiling. "Maurice," he says.

Maurice finally relents and shakes Jake's outstretched hand and says, "Jake."

I guess in man-speak, this means things are good until further notice.

No one says anything for a minute until I break the silence with, "Ah, thanks, Maurice. So I'll see you later?" I smile.

Maurice pauses another minute and then, "Right. I'm just inside the door here, Evie. You need me, you call, yeah?"

"Yeah, Maurice," I say softly.

Maurice closes the door to his apartment, and Jake looks back at me. He glances between my door and me and finally sighs, running his hand through his short hair again and furrowing his brow in that heart-stopping way he does. "Okay, I get it. I'm not invited in. Can I at least have your phone number, Evie?"

I pause. Oh, okay, why not? I like him. He's handsome and nice, and he makes me feel good in a way no one has in a really long time. Okay, if I'm truthful, maybe ever. Not since Leo . . . but I'm not going there. And that was eight years ago. I was a kid then. In my adult life, no one has affected me the way Jake Madsen affects me. I'm sure it's highly common in Jake World, but it is most definitely not in Evie World and it feels nice, exciting.

"Give me your phone," I say, and he hands it over. I program my number in and hand it back.

He grins at me, and then turns to walk away, saying, "I'm done stalking you, Evie. We've just elevated our status for real."

I laugh. "You take all the fun out of everything, you know that, Jake Madsen?" But I'm smiling like a loon, and as I catch his reflection in the front glass door, so is he. *Oh God, Jake Madsen is going to call me.* I really want Jake Madsen to call me. *Damn.*

CHAPTER SEVEN

Nicole picks me up a little after five, and I get in the passenger side of her small, silver Honda, a bottle of red wine and a plate of brownies in hand. Kaylee loves brownies, and I love Kaylee.

"You look all glowy," Nicole says, smiling over at me. "Using a new moisturizer or did you meet Prince Charming?"

I guess I'm silent for a beat too long before answering, "What? No. Probably just the cold air," because Nicole's mouth drops open and she sputters, "Oh my God! You totally did. You met a guy. Oh, wow. Oh, I've been waiting for this forever. Wait! Don't tell me anything yet. Mike needs to hear all the details."

"What? Nicole. Seriously. It's nothing. Actually," I frown, "what if it's nothing?"

Nicole is literally bouncing up and down in her seat, and she breaks about twenty different traffic laws speeding to her house.

When she pulls into her driveway, she hops out and although she's wearing red heels that look dangerous, she runs to my side and practically pulls me from the car, plucking the bottle of wine out of my hands.

She lets us in, and Kaylee immediately comes running to the door shrieking, "Auntie Evie! Auntie Evie!"

I catch her in my arms, laughing, and hug her to me. Then I pull back slightly and say seriously, "Kaylee, I didn't think it was possible, but you've gotten prettier. I'm worried about Cinderella's job security."

She's giggling. "No, Belle! I wanna be Belle!"

"Okay then, Belle is in serious trouble." I set her down gently and say in a whisper, "I brought brownies. Eat a good dinner and I'll give you the biggest one." I wink.

"Okay, Auntie Evie," she whispers back conspiratorially. And with that she runs off to continue playing with the Barbies she abandoned on the floor when I walked in the door.

Nicole, who had been checking on something that smells delicious in the oven, opens the bottle of wine I brought, grabs two glasses from her cabinet and begins pouring. "So spill," she says as Mike walks down the stairs, his hair still damp from a shower.

"Evie," he calls. "How are you?" He walks in the kitchen and gives me a quick hug. I love Mike. He's a nice guy, a good guy, one of the best.

"She's GREAT," Nicole interrupts. "She met a man. She's just about to give details. Come on. Let's sit."

"Seriously, guys," I say. "Nic, you're making too big a deal of this. He's just this incredibly gorgeous, funny guy who I met when he was stalking me last week." Then I plop down on their couch, set my wine down and pick up a People magazine on the coffee table and start idly flipping through it just to annoy them.

Nicole and Mike aren't sitting. They're standing in the middle of the living room staring at me.

"WHAT?" Nicole shrieks. "He was stalking you? Why? Wait! How did you know he was stalking you?" She frowns. "Was he really stalking you?"

Mike is silent, but he's looking at me like he might be slightly confused and slightly pissed. They both take seats on the loveseat across from me.

I put the magazine down and pick my wine glass back up.

I think of everything that's transpired in the last forty-eight hours and I suddenly feel overwhelmed. I take a big gulp of red wine and frown slightly. If I'm going to spill, then I guess I have to *spill*. "Well, here's the thing, I guess I have to start at the beginning, guys."

Nicole glances at her watch and looks back at me like I'm about to disclose where Jimmy Hoffa is buried. "Dinner will be ready in twenty minutes. Go." Their eyes are riveted on me. I really do love them both so much. I should have told them more about my background so long ago. I've just tried so hard to leave my past behind.

"You know I grew up in foster care," I start. "I've never really discussed why, but basically, my mom was a junkie who did whatever she needed to do to score a hit. She was never really concerned where I was, if there was any food in the refrigerator, or if I had any clean clothes. She also was never really concerned about who she was bringing around our apartment when she was partying, and that meant she didn't really care what kind of sickos she was exposing me to. In fact, she watched a couple times as things got seriously inappropriate with several of her boyfriends and me." I take another huge sip of wine. "Of course, she was so zoned out on those occasions, it's hard to say whether she was actually present or not. Luckily, I was able to make myself invisible for the most part when she was on one of her benders and the partying went on for days. I would hide in a closet, under the bed, or anywhere else I could fit my small body where I felt it would be safe." I glance up at Nicole and she looks stricken, tears glistening in her eyes. Mike has a hard look on his face, and his eyes are focused on Kaylee as she plays with her dolls in the open-plan dining room just out of hearing distance.

"Anyway," I sigh, "the police were finally called during one of her parties, and I was found in a compromising position with one of the wasted party-goers." Nicole gasps. Mike clenches his jaw.

"Oh, honey," Nicole whispers. I wave it off. It's been so long. It seems like a lifetime ago.

But if I'm truthful, other times it seems like yesterday. I take a moment to collect my thoughts and emotions.

"When I got to foster care, I met a boy named Leo almost immediately. We were only in the same home for a couple months, but we formed a bond, and it's hard to explain how strong that bond was to anyone who hasn't been in a situation where you feel like you're completely alone in the world at such a young age." I pause, lost in thought. "It wasn't just that we were in a similar situation, it was," I pause again, working out how to phrase the next part, "it was as if I had found my other half, and I finally felt complete. I know that sounds unfathomable being that I was only ten years old, but it's the truth, plain and simple. It was as if all of those ten painful years had been for the sole purpose of bringing me to that boy in that place and time, and so I could only be grateful for any pain that had transpired to lead me to him."

I look up at Nicole and Mike, and they're staring at me with matching expressions of shock. This is probably a record for the most words spoken about myself in a row over the last three years that I've known them. "Evie," Nicole breathes.

I smile gently at her and go on. "At first, we formed a connection as friends, and I almost thought of him as a big brother, a protector, but as the years went by and we grew older, we fell in love. And the thing about falling in love is that no matter where you are when it happens, you can't help but to color those moments with beauty, even if you're in a location of ugliness. He made what would have been a place of nightmares, into a place to dream.

"I was in and out of court, having to testify against my birth mom who never once showed up for the proceedings." I pause, letting the memory of that hurt wash over me. "He made it okay. When I was loved by Leo, I always felt like I would be okay." My own eyes well up now, and I have to gather myself to continue.

"He had moved to a different foster home a small distance away from mine, but he visited me as often as he could get away, and we always met on the roof outside my bedroom window. We dreamed together, we planned a life together. We were so young, but we were so sure." I can't help the smile that finds its way to my lips.

"When I was fourteen and he was fifteen, he was adopted by a couple. This was somewhat shocking as it's very, very rare for a teenager to be adopted. I didn't know much about the couple, but from what Leo told me, they were very kind, and they really just wanted to give a home to a kid who most likely had no hope of having one.

"I was thrilled for him, except for the fact that he found out his new adopted father had gotten a new job in San Diego and they'd be moving very quickly.

"We promised we would wait for each other, that he would come for me when I turned eighteen and that we would make a life together. He promised me that as soon as he got to San Diego, he would write to me with all his information and that we would keep in touch through letters. He asked me to promise him that I would save myself for him. I couldn't have imagined doing anything different anyway. In my mind and in my heart, I belonged to Leo, and he belonged to me. Distance would never change that."

"Jesus, honey," Nicole whispers, bringing her hand to her chest.

I sigh and continue. "He came to say goodbye to me the night before he left, and he kissed me for the very first time. And when I say he kissed me, I mean it was like a vow, that kiss. I've heard people say they lose themselves in a kiss, but it was like we found ourselves the second our lips met. It was like he took me apart and put me back together with that kiss."

I'm silent again, and when I snap to, I realize I'm touching my lips with my fingers. I pull them away and look back up at Nicole and Mike who are gawking at me. "Jesus, honey," she repeats, and really, there's nothing else to say.

I direct my eyes at Nicole and drop the bomb, "But he never did write to me from San Diego. I never heard from him again."

They're staring at me, stunned. "But—" Nicole starts.

"What—" Mike says.

I put my hand up. "I know. I've gone over every possible scenario in the past eight years, believe me. Anything you can think of, I checked into it. I didn't know his new adoptive parents' last name, so I didn't get far. There were so many things my fourteen-year-old self didn't think to ask. Of course, I had no idea I'd need any information that he'd be unable to give to me later. But I really did try to research whether there was a physical reason why he never contacted me. I came up empty each and every time."

"You were just kids, though, Evie," Nicole starts, and I stop her by shaking my head no vigorously. "No, I know we were kids, but these feelings were very, very real. For both of us. I can't explain why he abandoned me, why he lied to me, but I know that his feelings up to that point were very, very real. I will not talk myself out of that. I don't know why they changed, but I will not talk myself out of them existing at all." I bite my lip.

A loud buzz sounds from the kitchen, and Nicole jumps up to turn off the stove and is back on the couch in about thirty seconds, staring at me spellbound again.

"Anyway," I say, trying to boost the mood in the room. "That was eight years ago." I almost feel like I have to console them after the sad ending of that story.

Then I bring them up to speed on Jake and his connection to Leo, how I confronted him, and him showing up today and asking for my phone number.

"Holy hell!" Nicole yells. "Evie, it's fate, that's what it is. I mean, I'm sorry to hear about Leo." She looks at me sadly. "But Jake's gorgeous, you say?"

I burst out laughing. Only Nicole. She winks at me, letting me know it was her intention to make me smile.

"Yes, completely gorgeous. Inhumanly gorgeous. I have no idea why he'd want to spend any more time with me, but it seems like he does."

Nicole and Mike both are looking at me like I've got two heads. "Um, honey, have you looked in a mirror recently?" she asks gently. Mike is nodding.

Mike continues, "Evie, do you realize that when you came to our fourth of July grill out last summer, every single guy there called me the next day asking if I could set him up with you?"

I wave my hand at them as if brushing their words away. "Mike, you do know that you have some seriously strange friends, right?" I smile though.

Mike laughs. "I know. Us electricians are not known for our amazing social skills, and that was mostly who was at that party. But they are still men, Evie. And they do still have eyes."

Kaylee bursts into the room at this point, demanding dinner. And I have to admit, I'm hungry too. Apparently, *spilling* burns a lot of calories.

We all head to the kitchen, and Nicole takes the casserole out of the oven while I get drinks for everyone. The table is already set.

"Grab the salad from the fridge, hon," Nicole calls over to Mike and he grabs a bowl covered in plastic wrap before joining us with several bottles of dressing. We all sit down and say a quick blessing before dishing out the food.

During dinner, we chat casually, asking Kaylee about preschool and teasing her about her "boyfriend" Mason. It's fun and warm and it feels beautiful, like it always does. I wonder, as I always do when I come for dinner at Nicole and Mike's house, whether I'll ever have a family of my own. I hope so, but I don't allow myself to dream about that. It's safer not to. For now, sharing in their glow is enough.

After dinner, Nicole starts loading the dishwasher, and I offer to give Kaylee a bath and put her to bed. We head upstairs, and I fill the tub with warm water and bubbles, and we chatter and laugh as she gets clean.

As I'm toweling her off, she asks, "Auntie Evie, will you tell me a bedtime story? Your bedtime stories are the BEST!"

I smile, hugging her little towel-clad body to me. "Yes, sweets, but it's gotta be a quick one tonight because Aunt Evie is tired, and I have to work early tomorrow, okay?"

"Okay," she sings.

I help her put her nightgown on and brush her teeth, and then we snuggle into her bed, and I begin.

"Once upon a time there was a little girl who was so impossibly sweet, so *intensely* sweet, so *amazingly* sweet, that when someone kissed her, their lips would turn into a delicious flavor of candy."

"Did they turn hard like candy, Auntie Evie?" Kaylee asks, frowning slightly.

"No, not hard, just flavored, and a shade deeper than their natural color. It was not only delicious, but also lovely. Kaylee's eyes fill with delight.

"Her mom kissed her and her lips were the flavor of cherry vanilla. Her little sister kissed her and her lips were the flavor of bubblegum."

"But Auntie Evie, what if they didn't like the flavor of their lips?"

"Well, the flavor only lasted for about three months so it would wear off eventually. But everyone loved the flavor of their lips because somehow the flavor was linked to the chemistry in the particular person's body, and so it naturally came out just right each and every time."

Kaylee nods and snuggles closer.

"Well, eventually, word got out about this little girl and her unique ability, and people came from all around the world to kiss her and get their own candy-flavored lips. Pretty soon the crowds were so large, her parents had to start charging to keep the crowds down, and so they could afford to quit their jobs and set up a business they called *Candy Lips*."

Kaylee yawns and so do I.

"The little girl grew sadder and sadder because of all the people who came just to take from her, to use her for her ability, day after day after day. Her parents watched her grow more withdrawn and distant by the week, and their impossibly sweet little girl was withering before their very eyes."

Kaylee yawns again.

"So they moved to a distant country in the middle of the night and were never heard from again. Although there is a tribe of aboriginals in Australia who are said to have the rosiest, sweetest-looking lips on the continent."

I wink down at Kaylee and stand up so I can pull the covers up to her beautiful little face.

"You rushed that ending, Auntie Evie," she says, but she's smiling a sleepy smile. "I'm going to think of something even better."

I laugh. "Well, okay, little critic. I can't wait to hear it." I smile at her again, kiss her forehead and walk to the door. "Goodnight, little sweetness," I whisper as I turn out the light.

"Goodnight, Auntie Evie," I hear as I close the door.

CHAPTER EIGHT

Evie is Ten, Leo is Twelve

I'm walking to the usual cafeteria table in the back that I share with Willow, school lunch tray in hand, when I spot him, Denny Powell, the boy who never misses the opportunity to humiliate me. My eyes dart left and right, looking for a path that won't make it so I have to walk right past him. There isn't one. Also, he's spotted me, and if I turn and run, he'll make things even worse. Holding my head high and ignoring him as I walk past is my safest bet at this point.

I'm so intent on my mission of making it past him that I don't notice his foot sweep out just as I'm about to exhale with relief. I'm holding my tray out in front of me and so as my feet tangle with his leg, my weighted arms pull me forward. I crash down to the floor, mac 'n' cheese, steamed carrots, and Jell-O ending up all over my short-sleeved, yellow, button-down shirt, some splatters hitting my face and hair.

My body goes into survival mode, letting go of the tray, turning around and crab crawling backward, away from Denny, but through the spilled food. When I see he's still in his seat, barely containing the laughter that's just behind his eyes and in the smirk on his lips, I rise slowly to my feet, feeling as if I'm somewhere just outside my body.

I'm a mess of dripping food, milk puddling on the floor at my feet as the leaking carton empties its contents. I feel brittle as heat fills my cheeks, and tears pool in my eyes. The laughter has already started, and now more are joining as my eyes dart around in panic. Finally, Denny gives in and lets out a loud guffaw. I briefly note that it sounds nasally and high pitched. I make eye contact with a few people who are staring at me with pity in their eyes, and that's almost worse, so I look away from them quickly.

Suddenly, there's a hand on my arm, gripping me solidly, and I hear a boy's voice say quietly, "Come on, Evie, I'll walk you to get cleaned up." I look at the hand on my arm and then my eyes travel up as if in slow motion. It's Leo McKenna, the boy who moved into my foster home last month. He's in the grade above me, even though he had a birthday a couple weeks ago and turned twelve. I don't turn eleven for three more months. I nod jerkily, and move to step over the food at my feet, but Leo holds me in place. When I look back at his face, I see he's looking thoughtfully at Denny Powell. Denny notices, too, and demands, "What are YOU looking at?"

"I was just trying to picture what you'd look like if you had half a brain in your head. Maybe a little different around the eyes . . . hard to say. Requires a vivid imagination."

Denny jumps up, his face going red, clenching his fists, "What did—" But that's when we hear the sharp click-clack of heels hurrying toward the cafeteria. Denny stops where he is.

Leo looks around the room at large and says, "Anything can be funny as long as it's happening to someone else, right?" He makes a disgusted sound and then guides me to the door. The principal, Mrs. Henry, is just turning into the cafeteria, and Leo says, "Evie accidentally dropped her tray. I'm walking with her to the restroom."

"Oh, okay," she says, glancing at me worriedly. "I'll call the janitor to clean it up. You okay, dear?" she asks, and I just nod as we walk out, wondering why Leo didn't tell her what Denny did. I'm too embarrassed to say a word though.

Willow rushes up behind us in the hall, grabbing my elbow and whispering, "Evie, are you okay?" Willow always seems to be whispering, as if she thinks if she talks too loudly, she'll alert someone to her existence. I look down at her and give her a reassuring smile.

We leave Leo in the hall and go into the girls' restroom. I clean up my shirt with wet paper towels as best as I can and wipe the food splatters off my face and out of my hair. Then I stand in front of the blow dryer for a few minutes until my shirt is mostly dry. I sigh as I stand in front of the mirror, biting the inside of my mouth and looking at myself for several minutes. I know what everyone sees; bangs that are too long because no one takes me to get regular hair trims, old clothes that are getting too tight, the fact that I need a training bra (I'm too embarrassed to ask someone to buy one for me), and shoes that flap when I walk because the sole is coming loose.

My eyes move to the left to watch Willow looking silently at me, too. She smiles her shy Willow smile and says, "That boy likes you."

I raise my eyebrows. "Leo?" I smile back. "Nah, he just doesn't like Denny Powell."

"Probably not. But he still likes you." She grins.

I grin back and grab her hand as we leave the restroom.

Leo is standing against the wall across from the restroom with one leg bent, foot against the wall, and his hands shoved in his pockets. He smiles as the bell rings and says, "Come on, I'll walk you girls to class." Then he reaches into his backpack and pulls out a small bag of peanuts, hands them to me, and winks. My lunch.

****

I'm sitting on the front porch of my foster home after school doing my homework when Leo walks up the front path. My eyes widen as I realize he has a swollen, black eye and a bloody lip.

"Oh my God. What happened?" I whisper, standing and walking to him.

He grins, though, and so I stop, put my hands on my hips, and look questioningly at him.

"Leo, what exactly is funny about getting beaten up?"

"The fact that Denny Powell looks worse than I do."

"Leo! He's twice your size. He could have KILLED you. I can't believe you did that. Why?"

He purses his lips and looks at me as if he's irritated. "Because he had it coming, that's why."

I take a deep breath, reaching out to touch him, but then drawing back. "Your face, though. It looks painful." I grimace.

"This kind of pain is the easy kind," he says, and brushes past me, into the house.

I know what he means, too. I think of that saying, "Sticks and stones can break your bones, but names can never hurt you," and how it's all backward. Sticks and stones and fists CAN break your bones, but it's the words that break your heart.

CHAPTER NINE

The next day as I'm taking my break at work, I notice I have a missed call, and then I see a text from the same unknown number.

Call me when you get a minute, beautiful. JM

Oh gosh! It's Jake. And he called me beautiful. I suck in a quick, excited breath.

I dial his number nervously, and he picks up immediately with, "Evie."

"Hi, Jake." Why do I sound all breathy? *Damn.*

"Listen, I'm running into a meeting so I can only talk for a minute, but I'd like to take you to dinner tonight."

"Oh," I say, surprised. "Um, I—"

"Evie, it's a yes or yes question," he says teasingly.

I smile. "I—yes, that will work," I say, suddenly feeling shy and out of my element.

I can hear the smile in his voice when he says, "Great. I'll pick you up at seven."

"Um—" I stutter, stupidly.

"See you tonight, Evie," he says and hangs up before I can stutter into the phone any more than I already have.

Holy hell!

****

This is one of those times when I wish I had a tub. I'd freaking love to soak in a tub before my date with Jake. I'm not completely sure why. It just seems like something I should be doing before a date with Jake Madsen. *A date with Jake Madsen!*

I allow myself a moment of panic. I'm completely out of my comfort zone here. This doesn't feel safe at all. What if he tries to kiss me? Maybe I should cancel. I have no idea how to date.

I pull it together. It's just dinner. If I feel uncomfortable, I'll tell him I don't feel well and come home. Okay, I can do this.

I take a shower, shaving everywhere, and then moisturize completely, every inch. I take off my old toenail polish and brush on new candy-apple red on my toes.

While my toenail polish is drying, I dry my hair carefully, and then I take the curling iron to it until it's falling down my back in loose curls.

I take a little extra time with my makeup, brushing on mascara as usual, but also using a little bit of black eyeliner, blusher, and a sheer berry lip gloss.

I pull on a pair of black lace panties and a matching bra and then head over to my small closet.

I have no idea where Jake is taking me to dinner so I hemm and haww for several minutes over what to wear before finally texting Nicole.

Me: Date with Jake! What do I wear to dinner? Didn't tell me where we're going.

Nicole: What??? You owe me a shitload of details tomorrow. Black slacks, cream lace cami you wore to my bday dinner and your black strappy sandals. Black

wool coat over cami. But keep it off when you answer door. ;)

Me: K. You lifesaver. xxoo Talk tomorrow.

Nicole: Uh yeah we will. ;) Be good. Sneak a pic of Mr. Gorgeous for me. xxoo

Me: Bcuz that wouldn't be awkward at all.

:p

I pull on the outfit Nicole picked and look at myself in the mirror. The black slacks are tame enough, but the cream, lace cami is all kinds of sexy, and I fidget in front of the mirror, wondering if I can pull it off in front of Jake. It has spaghetti straps and an empire waist so it's fitted on my chest and then flares out, further accentuating the swell of my breasts.

I turn away from the mirror, taking a deep breath. I decide to open a bottle of wine and have a glass before Jake arrives, to give me courage and calm my nerves.

I've just taken my fourth sip of wine when I hear a knock on my door. It's 6:53 p.m.

I pour my unfinished wine down the drain and rinse my glass quickly before I walk to the door. Jake smiles at me as I swing it open. My eyes run over him and his dark gray slacks, button-down white shirt, black belt, and black dress shoes. *Oh my*. He walks in without being invited, and suddenly his hands are cupping my jaw and pulling me firmly to his body.

Hi.

There's a second where our eyes meet, and I register something animalistic and primal in his expression before his mouth crashes down on mine.

I make a noise at the back of my throat and lift my arms around his neck. My heart is beating furiously in my chest.

His tongue sweeps inside my mouth, and I whimper as my own tongue meets his.

God, he tastes so good. Is this really happening?

It's been a really long time since I've been kissed. And I've *never* been kissed like this.

My body presses into his to get more of him as his tongue plunders my mouth, our tongues dancing, drinking. It's delicious, demanding, and very, very hot.

One of my hands come up to his soft hair, and I run my fingers through it as one of his hands comes down to cup my ass, and this feels very, *very* good, so I whimper into his mouth again to which he moans into mine. I feel that moan as a bolt of arousal between my thighs.

My knees are weak as I cling to him. His kiss has become my anchor to this earth, the very reason for my existence.

So when he tears his mouth from mine, breathing hard and stepping back, I make a sound of protest in my throat, and my eyes slowly open to see Jake grinning down at me.

"Damn, you can kiss."

I smile shyly up at him, trying to get my bearings, breathing heavily, and with every inhale, draw his delicious woodsy scent inside me.

"Wow—" I say, stupidly. *That was, uh, unexpected . . . and completely thrilling.*

"Yeah," he says, grinning again. "Hungry?"

I blink up at him, and when his question registers, I say, "Yeah."

I lock up and shrug on my coat, and he walks me out to his car, parked in front of my building.

"Doesn't the norm dictate that you were supposed to kiss me *after* our date?" I ask, smiling up at him.

"Couldn't wait." He winks. "It was either kiss you, or go insane."

Wow, I like that. I smile at him.

Jake lets me in the passenger side of his BMW as I grin up at him like a fool. I sink into the buttery leather seat, inhaling the new car smell. I've heard about this but never actually experienced it. I understand what all the hype is about now. I lean my head back and close my eyes.

Mmmm, new car smell.

He closes my door and walks around the car and slides in, and now I'm breathing in new car smell and Jake's delicious woodsy scent. *Yum.* As he pulls out onto the street, he takes my left hand in his and brings it to his lips. Then we hold hands between our seats as he drives with his left hand.

"So, where are you taking me?" I ask, smiling.

"Do you like seafood?" he asks. "I thought we'd go to a restaurant on the river."

"Yes, I love seafood. Sounds nice."

We drive in companionable silence for a few minutes before my wheels start turning. I decide I need to know exactly what Jake Madsen's intentions are when it comes to me.

I already feel like Jake holds all the power here and I know he's way out of my league, and despite knowing that, I am sitting in his car letting him take me out to dinner. I'm not a girl who's willing to take a lot of chances in life. That's who I am, who I have to be. And this man already has me all off balance—all giddy and thrilled—and I've only known him a week. I love it and I hate it all at once.

I realize that Jake Madsen is the type of man that women want to call their own. I'm not immune. But I'm not stupid, either.

"So, Jake," I say, biting my lip, "do you date a lot?"

"No." Then he pauses, thinking, and goes on, "There have been a lot of women, Evie, but no, I didn't date many of them." He glances at me, gauging my reaction to that snippet of information, and then turns back to the road. "I'm not proud of that, but it's the truth. Does that bother you?" He seems troubled.

I'm not completely sure why Jake shared this with me, but I have an idea and it's not good. I remain as expressionless as possible when I say, "Jake, I can't be your fuck buddy."

He doesn't look at me when he says, "I don't want that with you, Evie."

My stomach plummets to my feet. *Oh, shit! I'm an idiot!*

"Oh. I just thought . . . I mean, I . . . Because . . ." I stutter. *Oh God, Can I please die now?*

"Evie," he says quietly, finally looking at me, "what I mean is, when I fuck you, you're going to be mine. Is that clear enough for you?"

Oh!

My eyes widen as I stare straight ahead, not knowing what to say. His words, unbelievably arrogant as they are, are shooting electricity straight between my legs. I clench my thighs together, feeling confused by my reaction.

"Evie, look at me. You feel this, too, don't you?"

And Jake is right because I know exactly what he means. The sparks between us are practically tangible. I have never felt this kind of physical heat and longing for another person. Not ever.

I nod at Jake. "Yes," I whisper, feeling like I've just agreed to something, but I'm not sure exactly what.

He smiles over at me as he pulls into a parking spot in front of a restaurant called "The Chart House."

He shuts off the car and turns to me. His beautiful face is serious as he says, "Can I ask how many men you've dated, Evie?" He seems to be holding his breath.

I'm caught off guard and I feel my cheeks flame. I look forward and say flippantly, "So many men, Jake, but I doubt you'd say I actually *dated* many of them."

His nostrils flare, and anger fills his eyes for a brief moment before he schools his expression and looks at me silently. "You're fucking with me," he finally says softly.

"It's okay for you but not for me?" I ask.

"Yes, because you're a better person than I am," he says simply, like it's the most obvious thing in the world.

"Jake," I start. But I'm not sure what to say. He might think he knows what kind of girl I am. I'm sure my inexperience oozes off me. But what he doesn't know is that I've never been enough for anyone. No one who I've needed has ever wanted to keep me.

"I just want an honest answer. I just want to know how many men have been in your life." His jaw is hard. *And what the hell?* What business is this of his? Still, I asked him and he was honest with me.

I sigh. "I've dated a couple guys, mostly set-ups by my friend Nicole. No one seriously and no one more than three times. The last guy I went out on a date with was a year ago. We went out for dinner once. He asked if he could take me out again, I declined. Is that specific enough for you?" I feel embarrassed and irritated that he insisted on this information because spelling it out makes me realize how pathetic my social life is.

He takes my hand in his. "And in high school?" he asks.

"High school?" I shake my head slightly and laugh a hollow sounding laugh. "No, I didn't date in high school."

He gazes at me for a moment, something both fierce and tender in his expression. Then he leans over and turns my head toward him with one finger on my jaw and kisses me sweetly on the lips.

"Time for me to feed you. And talk about lighter stuff. I want to see you smile and hear you laugh. I want to know who Nicole is, I want to know what your favorite movie is, why you love to run so early in the morning, and what music is on your iPod. Wait there."

He comes over to my side of the car, opens the door for me, and lets me out. He takes my hand and we head inside.

****

The restaurant is beautiful, with a lovely view of the river, the food delicious, and we laugh and talk through dinner. I tell him about Nicole, Mike, and Kaylee. I talk about what running means to me, about how I grew up feeling powerless and how running makes me feel strong and accomplished, a feeling I revel in. He nods like he understands this.

He seems to be interested in everything I'm saying and nods and smiles, encouraging me to continue. He makes me feel comfortable and interesting.

"You've done really well, Evie," Jake tells me.

I frown slightly. What is he talking about? "I'm a hotel maid, Jake," I say, as if he doesn't already know this.

"Don't ever be ashamed of the honest work you do to pay the rent. It's damn rare that someone who comes from the background you do, doesn't go on to repeat the cycle . . . drugs, early pregnancy, domestic abuse. Be proud of yourself. You deserve all the respect in the world. I think you're incredible," he says, looking at me with beautiful warmth in his brown eyes.

No one has ever told me they were proud of me. Not one single person. And so this affects me deeply, and I feel wetness in my eyes. I look down, embarrassed, and take a sip of my wine.

"Thank you," I whisper.

We're quiet for a minute and although I don't really feel like going into any details about my and Leo's past, the curiosity is too much for me. I was in shock about Leo's death the last couple times I was with Jake, but this time, I find myself asking, "Can I ask you about Leo?"

His eyes snap up to mine and he nods. "Of course." But he sounds a little wary all of a sudden.

"Was *he* happy? Did he have a good life?"

He pauses. "I don't know how to answer that. I didn't know him very well. I mean, outside of sports and partying, that sort of thing."

I nod. I realize I'm biting the inside of my mouth, a bad habit I thought I'd left behind in foster care. I stop and take a deep breath. "When he left, he promised he'd keep in touch and he never did. Do you have any idea why?"

He looks sad, like he feels sorry for me, and that's exactly why I didn't want to bring this up, but I feel like I have to know.

"I'm sorry. I don't. I don't really know what his home life was like.

And the first time he talked about you to me was in the hospital, and I've told you the extent of what he said."

I nod, taking another sip of my wine. I feel like bringing Leo's name up has thrown a melancholy over our date that wasn't there before, and so I rally, smile at Jake and say, "This might be a little bit of an odd thing to say, but, well, if he was going to send anyone, I'm glad it was you. I've had a nice time tonight."

He's silent for a second, a strange expression on his face, but then he smiles warmly and says, "I'm glad he sent me, too. I thought I was doing him a favor, but it looks like he did *me* a favor."

After our plates are cleared, Jake reaches across the table and takes my hands, and says, "Can I take you out again?"

I nod yes, looking down and feeling shy.

The waiter returns Jake's credit card, and he quickly signs the receipt and says, "Ready?" as he starts to stand up.

I smile and stand up, too. He helps me on with my jacket, grabs my hand again, and we exit the restaurant.

We drive back to my apartment, chatting easily about the city and some of our favorite spots. He tells me a little bit about growing up near the beach and when I tell him I'd love to see the ocean someday, he grabs my hand and tells me he'd love to be the one to take me there.

I don't answer, thinking it's a little soon to be making plans that involve travel.

We drive the last couple of miles in companionable silence, the radio playing softly in the background.

We pull up a half a block down from my apartment because the spaces in front are all taken, and Jake shuts off the car, but he doesn't get out. He looks over at me, and I smile at him. I feel like we're cocooned away from the world in his warm car, just the two of us.

"You are so beautiful when you smile," Jake says.

Suddenly, he's leaning over and taking my jaw in his hand as he gently brushes his lips over mine.

He leans his forehead against mine and looks right into my eyes.

There is an unreadable expression there, and my heart starts to beat faster as we stare at each other, mere centimeters away. I don't know whether I'm scared or whether his closeness is causing my blood to pump faster. I don't know what I'm feeling in this moment, don't know whether I want to move even closer or pull away. It's all so intense, and so soon. I shake my head very slightly and, in the end, I pull away.

"What's wrong?" he asks, and his voice is quiet, gentle.

I exhale. "Nothing, this is just all kind of new for me." But I smile at him and he smiles back.

Jake walks me to my apartment door, and although he started the night with a passionate kiss, he ends it with a kiss that is almost chaste, brushing his soft lips across mine, smiling his beautiful smile, and leaving me at my open door, disappointed and wanting more. But aside from throwing myself at him—which I would absolutely never do—my only choice is to smile and watch him walk away.

CHAPTER TEN

The next morning, I wake up early to go on a run. I do a quick three miles around the park. The morning is crisp and cold, the sky a mixture of yellow, orange, and soft blue.

I return home, and as I go to open the front lobby door, I notice the lock has been fixed. Finally! But then I frown, staring suspiciously at it. Wait, is it a coincidence that Jake got all pissy about it a couple days ago and today it's magically fixed?

I head inside wondering and take a quick shower, singing along with the small radio I leave on my bathroom sink. I dry off and pull on my Hilton uniform. I have an early shift today and I work a catering job tonight. It's a party at one of the swankier hotels downtown, and it always pays well and so I never pass those jobs up if I'm offered one.

I dry my hair quickly and pull it into a low, loose bun at the nape of my neck. Some light makeup and I'm ready to head out. As I grab my phone off the kitchen counter, I notice I have a text message from Jake. I smile before I even read it.

Jake: I had a great time with you last night. What are you doing today?

I grin and type back quickly.

Me: I had a really good time too. :) Working both jobs. Won't be home until late.

I grab my coat and head out. As I walk out the front lobby door, I'm reminded of the newly fixed lock and follow up my message quickly with:

Me: btw, know anything about the lock repair on the front door of my building?

I take a seat on the bus and a minute later my phone dings.

Jake: I may have called and threatened your landlord with legal action if he didn't do door repair. Glad he stepped up. You should always feel safe.

I read his message over again and my heart warms. Damn. I like him. A lot. Will this end well? I sit chewing on the inside of my mouth for a minute, considering this completely unexpected situation. Jake's clearly way out of my league. Nothing about him makes sense and everything screams risk. For me, hoping for things feels scary. But he seems to really like me, too, and he says he feels the same electricity between us that I do. *Just relax, Evie, you've gone on one date.* And now I've just talked myself into a sour mood. Finally, I reply:

Well, thanks. I appreciate it.

A couple minutes go by before I get another text.

Jake: Anything for you. Headed in to a meeting. Have a good day/night at work. Can I call you tomorrow?

Sigh.

Me: What if I say no?

Jake: I'll call you anyway. ;) Have a good day, Evie.

I smile again and drop my phone in my bag. I'm not going to overthink this. *I'm totally going to overthink this.* But not right now. Right now I'm almost at work and I have back-to-back jobs. *Focus, Evie.*

I finish up my shift at the Hilton and hop the bus back home with plenty of time to take a quick shower. Why wash my hair again when I'm just going to be in and out of a kitchen all night and end up smelling like food anyway? I lay down for an hour to nap. I'll be out late tonight so I like to get at least an hour of sleep beforehand if possible.

I pull on a pair of PJs and head to the kitchen to make a sandwich for dinner. I put together a simple turkey, cheese, and lettuce sandwich and cut up an apple and eat standing at the kitchen counter.

Then I head to my bed, set the alarm for six o'clock and lie down. I fall asleep thinking about Jake.

My alarm goes off and I drag myself up. I feel like I could sleep for the rest of the night. But an hour will have to do for now. I pull on my catering uniform, a pair of black slacks and a white button-up shirt that's ironed and hanging in my closet. I fold my half apron neatly and put it in my purse.

I brush my hair out and put it back in the low bun I was wearing earlier. I wash my face and brush my teeth and apply a minimal amount of makeup, but go a little darker on the lipstick. After all, this is an evening party and even though I'm working there, I still think I can dress up my face a little bit.

The event doesn't start until eight, but my boss, Tina, likes us to get there an hour early to help set up and load the trays. I head out right at six fifteen, leaving plenty of time to bus it back downtown. I'll get a ride home from one of the other servers after the event ends.

I enter by the back door of the hotel where the event is being held as Tina has instructed, and head to the banquet room and the kitchen beyond.

"Evie!" I hear my name shrieked and grin immediately. I would know Landon's voice anywhere. I look up and there he is, fast-walking toward me through the banquet room, all sashaying hips and waving arms. Landon is hilarious, flamboyantly gay, and I love him to death. He picks me up and spins me around yelling, "God, I missed you! It's been WAY too long, Fancy Face! The phone is just no substitute. How the hell have you been?"

I'm laughing out loud as he sets me down. "Hey, you're the one who deserted me," I tease. But then I look over at him seriously as we begin walking toward the kitchen. "How's your mom?"

He sighs dramatically. "I left her complaining vehemently about how the woman who came in to clean her house while she was in the hospital did a piss-poor job of it. I think I can safely say that she's just fine."

Landon had traveled back to his hometown in Missouri to help out when his mom's MS landed her in the hospital two months ago. He's an only child and his mom and he are extremely close, she accepts him completely, and there is nothing he won't do for her. It's a beautiful thing.

"That's great to hear, Lan," I say. I look up at him and smile, taking in his blond good looks.

"And what has my little Fancy Face been up to while I've been gone?" he asks, opening the double doors to the massive hotel kitchen.

"Oh, you know, a little of this, a little of that. Working, reading, running, crushing on a really hot guy." I start to walk away knowing I'll be pulled back. I'm pulled back.

"What?" he shrieks, and no one does shrieking quite like Landon. Everyone working in the kitchen looks over at us, rolling their eyes before looking back at their tasks.

He grabs my arm and leads me over to a small desk in the corner where there's a sign-in board. I sign my name quickly and turn to Landon saying, "It really is just early. I, uh, ran into him recently and he's a friend of a friend and well, we went on one really great date, and he's completely hot, and that's really the extent of it. But I just have this gut feeling, you know?" I frown. "Wait, damn, I'm not supposed to say that out loud, am I? I've jinxed things now."

Landon's listening to me intently, and he's quiet for a minute after

I've stopped speaking, one finger on his lips, his hip cocked and gazing thoughtfully at me. Finally, he says, "Listen, Fancy Face. I've known you for almost four years now, and in all that time, I have never once heard you even *mention* a guy, or a girl. I would have taken either." I laugh. "So," he goes on, "this is momentous. This is huge. This has made my night. I know you putting yourself out there isn't easy." He looks at me sadly. "And I know you have good reasons for that. But whether or not this turns into anything, I swear to you, Evie, I'm just glad to know that you're willing to take a chance."

God, I really love Landon.

"Thanks, Lan," I say, slightly embarrassed.

"And by the way, saying something out loud doesn't jinx it, or else I would be constantly shouting about how donuts go straight to my ass. Damn, I'm addicted to Krispy Kreme. Can't stay away."

I laugh loudly.

He smiles that huge Landon smile for me and then says, "Also, I learned something when I was back home. Apparently, I'm a cliché."

I look confused. "What do you mean, a cliché?" I ask.

"You know, a cliché . . . the boss boinking his secretary, a cliché!"

"Yeah, I know what a cliché *is*, what do you mean you *are* one?"

"Oh, right. Well, I spent a lot of time at my mom's house while she slept, and she reads all these romance novels. So I read several and evidently, it's a *thing*, the beautiful girl with a gay best friend. It's a cliché. I'm a cliché."

I burst out laughing. "Ah, okay, well, it works. I guess because of my unequalled beauty, I can only hang around men who aren't tempted to molest me hourly. You're my only choice." I wink at him, slapping him on his ass.

Landon laughs, too, squealing as I smack him.

An hour later, the kitchen is in full swing. Tina, a really nice woman in her fifties with a head full of frizzy blonde curls and a great laugh, has greeted all of us and is helping load the trays. She owns the catering company, is a great boss—fair and helpful—with a wonderfully witty sense of humor.

I walk the floor of the ballroom, offering appetizers to the exquisitely decked-out guests. Women in long, beautiful evening gowns, and men in handsome tuxes. This event is a benefit to help raise awareness about autism spectrum disorders, so I can't help but to have a soft spot for these partygoers. I smile extra big as I offer Tina's delicious appetizers, moving around the room from guest to guest.

I've been around the room with three trays, when I rush back into the kitchen to fill another one.

Landon is next to me at the long, stainless steel counter, filling his own tray. "Girl, did you clock hottie in the far corner by the bar? Serious meltdown every time I catch a glance. True story."

I laugh. "I don't think I've made it that far. I keep running out of food mid room. I'll start over there this time, though." I wink, and he grins.

I walk back out on the floor and head over to the bar area, so that I can report back to Landon later. I stop at a small group, smiling as I offer them napkins and hold my tray out to them. It's filled with thin wafers, each holding a glob of black caviar. It looks dreadful to me, but these people are clearing my tray, so what do I know?

As I move away from them, I see the man Landon must be talking about. He has his back to me, but even from this viewpoint, I can tell that he's good-looking, all broad shoulders, slim waist and excellent backside. Too bad for Landon, though, there's a blonde in a red dress glued to his arm. I make my way closer and as the couple turns toward me, I inhale an audible gasp. It's Jake. Oh No!

Damn! Shit! Shit! Shit!

My heart plummets to my feet, and I stand stock still for a minute, weighing my options for escape. Too late, Jake spots me, and his eyes are surprised for a second, and then this unbelievable warmth floods them, and he smiles like I'm an old friend he hasn't seen in a decade.

God! I am such an idiot. I close my eyes very briefly and try to gather myself together, shooting him a smile I really hope looks as fake as it feels. Disappointment and hurt grip my heart.

"Evie," he says, disengaging himself from red dress and coming toward me, a look of concern on his face. "I didn't know you'd be here." His eyes are wide and glued to me.

God, he's gorgeous.

He's also a playing, lying *asshole*.

Before I can utter a word, red dress follows him saying, "Jakey, do you *know* her?" The pissy tone of her voice does not escape me.

And Jakey? Shit! Shit! Shit! I groan internally.

I glance at red dress and it sucks that despite the fact that she's pissy, I can't deny she's also stunning. Her dress looks like it cost more than my entire wardrobe put together, including my shoes and jackets. Then I look back at Jake and whisper stupidly, "Hi." God, I'm such an idiot!

Jake clenches his jaw, and although he's talking to red dress, his eyes are still riveted on me as he says, "Yes, I do know her. This is Evie Cruise." Almost as an afterthought, he cocks his head at red dress and says, "This is Gwen Parker."

My eyes cut back to Gwen and I whisper, "Hi." And again, I whisper it stupidly.

Gwen crosses her arms in front of her large, plastic-looking breasts and says, "I don't need an introduction, Jakey. I was just surprised that you know her." Then she hooks herself back onto Jake's arm and glares at me.

Jake takes a deep breath, his jaw ticks again, and he does not look happy. I guess it sucks to be caught as the phony asshole you are.

I'm shaking now, and I need to get far, far away from Jake and Gwen. And by far, I mean like, *Mexico*.

"Right," I say. "Well, have a nice evening." And then I start to turn away from them, but because I'm shaking, my tray tips forward, and one wafer slides off the edge before I can right it and said wafer, full of an extra large glob of black caviar, plops loudly onto Gwen's beautiful, silver, strappy sandal.

For a second, no one makes a sound, and I'm frozen in horror. Then, Gwen screeches, "Oh my God! Do you know how much these shoes cost? No, of course you don't! These are fourteen-hundred-dollar shoes!"

And oh my God, I'm frozen, but it registers I didn't even know fourteen-hundred-dollar shoes *existed* and that my estimation about my entire wardrobe equaling the cost of her outfit was way, *way* off. And not in my wardrobe's favor.

Landon rushes up to us seemingly from out of nowhere and takes my tray out of my hands, putting his face close to mine briefly as he leans in to take it, eyes wide, and says while barely moving his lips, "You okay, Fancy Face?"

I nod slightly to him and then bend down with Gwen where she's using a napkin to try to clean the caviar off her shoe, swearing under her breath. "I'm so sorry," I say. "Please, let me help you clean it off. If you'll come with me to the ladies room, I can use a cleaning cloth on it. I bet it will come right off."

She glares back at me, but she starts standing anyway and hisses, "Fine."

Jake is standing there watching this, his jaw clenching, and if that goes on much longer, he's going to need a mouth guard because from what I've heard, TMJ is no joke.

Landon rushes up again, offering Jake a glass of champagne from a tray of glasses, and I lead Gwen toward the ladies room.

Once we're there, I motion for her to sit on the chaise lounge, and she removes her shoe and hands it to me with a scowl. I open a small Bounce packet from the complimentary guest basket on the bathroom counter and wipe the top of the shoe off completely. I also offer Gwen a baby wipe from the guest basket so that she can thoroughly clean the top of her foot.

When I'm done, I hand her shoe back to her and say, "Good as new. I'm really very, very sorry. I hope I haven't put a dent in your evening." I'm just being nice. Truthfully, I hope I put a big dent in her evening because the feeling is mutual.

She ignores my comment, straps her shoe back on, and then heads to the sink to wash her hands, as I wash mine in the sink next to her. "You know," she says finally, "Jake loves a good cause. I can see why he's friends with someone like you."

She dries her hands and then turns around. "It's sweet really. Just don't get any ideas, okay? He's in my bed at the end of the day and *I'm* the one screwing his brains out."

With that, she brushes past me, knocking me to the side a little and walks out the door.

I will not cry. I will not cry.

Damn, Leo. Why did you send *him*? He totally played me. All that talk about *do you feel it, too, Evie* this and *you're so amazing, Evie* that and *God*! He has a girlfriend! And that thought makes me want to cry again. I stand against the bathroom wall, taking deep breaths and getting a handle on my emotions before I exit the bathroom.

I head back toward the kitchen. Landon is there and he pulls me aside whispering, "Holy SHIT, Evie, that's HIM, isn't it? Like *him*, him. Holy SHIT, he was, like, pacing the floor after you took off to the bathroom with Bitchy Barbie. Honey, the look on his face was *tragic*. WHAT is going on?"

I sigh as I take his hand and pull him over to the tray-stocking counter. "Obviously he has a *girlfriend,* Landon. He was probably shitting bricks that we'd both find out what a douchebag he is. Obviously I'm just an idiot who got all swoony about a guy after one date and some sweet words. When all along, he was just . . . I don't even know *what* he was doing. This is exactly why I do *not* need this type of thing. God, that was humiliating!" I frown and close my eyes briefly before looking back at Landon.

He looks at me sadly and squeezes my hand. "Evie, remember what I said to you earlier. No matter how this ends, I am fucking thrilled you put yourself out there. Do you hear me, Fancy Face?" He takes my face in his hands and looks at me for a minute and then whispers, "God, so fucking beautiful. No wonder Devil in Red was shooting eye darts at you."

I smile a real smile at Landon because he is seriously *so sweet*, and squeeze his hand back. "Hey, do you think it'd be okay with everyone if I stock trays back here instead of working the room?"

"Yeah, I think everyone would be fine with that. Plus, cocktail hour is almost over. Dinner is about to be served. Why anyone wants to eat dinner at nine at night is beyond me but I guess when you're the type of people who can afford fourteen-hundred-dollar shoes, you can make your own rules."

"Oh my God! You *heard* that?" I say, incredulously, loading a tray up with delicious-looking phyllo dough pockets.

"I did, but honey, I saw some strappy sandals that were nicer at Payless Shoe Source last week for twenty-nine bucks. I was gonna buy them but they didn't come in my size."

I burst out laughing. Landon winks at me and heads out the door.

I spend the rest of the night in the kitchen, loading up trays with the dinner courses for the other servers.

I'm loading up desserts when Tina breezes in saying, "Evie, darling! I heard you dropped caviar on the tall, blonde in red's foot!"

I freeze. Oh no. I turn slowly toward Tina and cringe. "I did, Tina. It was just an accident. I cleaned it for her and it came out completely."

"Honey," she continues, smiling a mischievous-looking smile, "do I look upset? That one looks particularly vapid. I'm just sorry you didn't score both feet." She squeezes my shoulder and rushes off.

I let out a relieved breath. *God, Tina is so great.*

Once dinner is served, including coffee, we servers are free to leave. There's another cleanup crew and they're in full swing in the kitchen now.

I'm washing my hands at the industrial kitchen sink when Landon walks back in. I notice he has a small frown on his face as he walks over to me and so I say, "What?"

"Dreamboat slipped this to me and asked that I give it to you. He said to tell you that they're his new favorite. And it must be said, Evie, he's hot, but he's *strange*." Then he hands me a mint and I recognize them from the complimentary bathroom baskets.

I furrow my brow, looking at the plain white wrapper of the mint lying in my hand. Then I turn it over and I can't help it as my frown turns into a smile. On the other side of the small package, it says in bold print, *World's Greatest Mints.*

I stare at it for a few seconds, not knowing exactly what to think. Finally, I chuck it in the trash and go back to work.

CHAPTER ELEVEN

Evie is Twelve, Leo is Thirteen

I'm lying on the roof outside my room, staring up at the clear, summer sky. I love looking up at the stars because they make me believe that some things in this world are permanent.

I moved into this foster home a year ago and I like it here well enough. My new foster parents have three of us living here, but I have my own room because there's a set of sisters and they share one. My space is small—an old transformed laundry room—but it has a window that opens out onto a very gently sloping portion of the roof, and I love to come out here and lay under the sky.

My foster parents are clearly fostering for the checks they get for our care, but they're not mean people, just mostly disinterested in us, which is fine by me. Ideal, even.

A small stone hits the roof next to me and I smile. It's Leo's sign that he's coming up.

I hear him climb the trellis, and then he's crawling across the roof, and he plunks himself down next to me, reclining like I am. He's wearing baggy athletic shorts and I take in his knobby boy knees.

I look over at him and he's frowning.

"What's wrong, Leo?" I ask.

His face gets angry and he says, "What did I do to make him hate me so much, Evie, other than exist?"

I roll toward him, bending my arm and resting my head in my hand. "Leo—"

But he interrupts me, saying, "He sent my brother to live in that hell hole just to hurt me. It wasn't even about Seth, it was about ME. He hurt an innocent little boy because he hates me so much he can't see straight."

My eyes fill with tears because I know he's right. I've learned over the two years I've known Leo that his dad is evil personified. Leo's big mistake was that his mom cheated on his dad and got pregnant with him. And because of Leo's grievous sin, being CREATED, his dad made it his mission in life to make Leo suffer.

Leo's second mistake was that he loved his younger brother, Seth, diagnosed with a severe form of autism and developmentally delayed. Because Leo's dad knew Leo loved Seth, he used him to hurt Leo. He threw beer cans at Seth's head, he let him wallow in his own waste all day while Leo was at school, unable to take care of him, and he was all-around cruel to Seth as a way to make a point to Leo. The sickest part of it was that Seth was his own flesh and blood, but all he saw him as was a pawn to use against the personification of his rage and humiliation.

"They put Seth in a state-run home." I hear the tears in his voice so I move closer and meld my body to his, and take his hand in mine. "That place will kill him."

The reason Leo's in foster care is because his dad beat the crap out of him after Leo tried to smother him in his sleep when his dad threatened to send Seth away. He had admitted to me that he knew he wouldn't have gone through with it, but he was so filled with fear and rage about him sending Seth away, that he wanted to divert his dad's wrath back onto himself. I've told Leo a thousand times how brave he is, but he doesn't believe me.

He sighs. "I don't even care what happens to me. I just don't want Seth to pay the price for it, and now he is because my mom signed the papers to have Seth put away, even though I know it was that douchebag's idea so he could move home. And I'm sure sticking it to me was a happy side benefit."

I don't say it, but the truth of the matter is, with Leo gone, caring for Seth is probably too much work for them. Leo had done everything for that little boy, from changing his diapers to playing with him, bathing him, and getting him to bed every night before he was sent to foster care.

"At court today, that son of a bitch passed me in the hall and whispered, 'Seth's GONE, boy. Hope he makes it.' Then he laughed his ass off as he walked away. Laughed, Evie! And my mom's no better. She just drags after him like he has her hypnotized with his charming personality." Tears are running down his cheeks now and I'm squeezing his hand like it's my lifeline.

"You know the only reason they even showed up at court today was to whine to the judge about what a sorry hand they were dealt in life to have a good-for-nothing kid like me for one, and a retard for the other. Maybe they thought the judge would feel so sorry for them, he'd spring for a tropical vacation or something." He laughs a miserable, hollow-sounding laugh.

"The thing is, Evie, I tried so hard to protect Seth, but in truth, I'm such a fuck up, I couldn't even manage that. The bastard is right about me. I ruin everything. I do something to ruin all the people who love me. Eventually, I fuck up everything because that's who I am."

And that's when I've had enough. "Stop," I say gently, but then firmer, "Stop! You're wrong, Leo. And I will not let that poor excuse for a human being make you think of yourself that way. You're brave and strong and noble. You're my Leo."

Leo's quiet now, breathing evenly, but his body is still tense. "Tell me a story, Evie," he says finally.

I take a deep breath and impossibly, move even closer to him. It's a hot summer's night and I'm already clammy from our closeness, but I don't move away.

We're both silent for several minutes, but eventually, I roll onto my back and say, "There was once a very beautiful woman, and although she had the face of an angel, she was empty on the inside. Right in the place where her heart should have been located, there was just a big, gaping hole. Because of this defect, an ogre, as ugly on the inside as he was on the outside, was able to court her and she married him.

"One day, the woman needed to get away from the ogre because his ugly personality and his ugly face became too much for her to bear, and as it turned out, even empty people can only take so much ugliness.

"She walked and walked until she came upon a quiet meadow, and she lay down in the middle of that meadow, soaking in the stillness of the night. What she didn't know was that there was a great beast lurking nearby, a massive lion, with a mane of gold and the thunderous roar of a hundred lions.

"As the beautiful, but empty woman lay in the field, this beast approached her quietly, and when she opened her eyes and spied him, she was spellbound because the sight of him was like nothing she had ever seen. He held the woman down with one massive paw, although, strangely, she wasn't scared, only curious. When dawn broke, the beauty awoke and thought that the night before had been only a dream. But the woman was now carrying a child, a son. And this beautiful boy would have the gifts of both his parents, the beauty of his mother and the heart of his father, the heart of a lion."

We're both quiet for several long moments.

Then Leo rolls toward me and he's looking at me with fire in his eyes. "I love you, Evie," he whispers.

"I love you, too, my Leo," I whisper back.

CHAPTER TWELVE

Landon gives me a ride home. He asks me repeatedly if I want to go out for late night drinks, but I really just want to crawl into my bed and shut out the world.

I never did see Jake again after the caviar incident, but it's for the best as far as I'm concerned. Watching him with Gwen would just have been even more painful and humiliating. And a further reminder of how gullible I'd been.

As Landon drops me off, he gives me a hug and tells me to call him tomorrow. "I have layers of dust all over my apartment and loads of laundry to do, but if you need any company, I'll drop all that excitement in a heartbeat." He smiles and I smile back. "Love you, girl," he says quietly.

"Love you, Lan," I say as I get out.

I unlock the front building door and of course my mind goes straight to Jake. Thinking about what he and Gwen are doing right about now just makes me cringe.

I let myself in to my apartment and take a quick shower. Then I brush my teeth, pull on an old T-shirt and a pair of shorts, and climb into bed.

I should have known that a beautiful, confident, successful man like Jake Madsen—who can have any girl he wants—would not choose a girl like me.

I curl around my pillow and finally let myself cry.

LEO (A SIGN OF LOVE NOVEL)

****

I wake up early the next morning and again drag myself out of bed. I shower, pull on my Hilton uniform, and dry my hair before putting it up in a ponytail. I put on a minimal amount of makeup and leave my apartment to catch the bus.

My shift goes by quickly as it usually does, and by noon, my mood has improved. I was fine before Jake Madsen interrupted my life, and I'll be fine after. I've lived through worse, much worse.

I exit through the employee door and am walking down the block toward the bus stop when a dark silver BMW pulls up next to me. I look over and there's Jake, smiling out at me and leaning across the passenger seat. My heart lurches and starts beating a mile a minute, but I keep my face blank. "Want a ride, little girl?" he asks, raising his eyebrows.

"Funny. No, Jake. I'm good with the bus." I keep walking.

"Evie, we need to talk," he says, but I keep walking.

Is he high?

"No, Jake, we don't," I say without looking in his direction, and because there are cars parked along the street from this point forward, Jake would be forced to pull to the side and get out of his car in order to keep talking to me. Which he does. *Damn.*

I sit down at the bus stop, and Jake jogs up to me. "Evie," he frowns. "Listen, last night was not what you think it was."

"Jake," I interrupt him from going any further. "It's been a long day. I'm really asking you to just leave this, okay? You should have told me you have a girlfriend. You didn't. It's done. Walk away." With that I turn around. The bus is coming.

"Gwen is not my girlfriend, Evie. I hope you'd think more of me than that after the time we've spent together."

Okay, girlfriend, fuck buddy, whatever. I'm just really not up for this. "Jake, again, walk away."

"I'm not gonna do that, Evie," he says quietly from behind me.

And now I'm just angry. I'm so damn tired, and just *angry*. I've spent the day cleaning up after slobs who think they can be just as disgusting as they please because someone lower than them will be there to wipe up their mess and I am just so. Damn. Tired. Just the fact that Jake Madsen ever darkened my doorway suddenly has me seething. I was doing FINE! And now, here he is in his stupid *Beemer*, in his stupid suit, with his stupid girlfriend/fuck buddy, whatever, in her fourteen-hundred-dollar shoes who thinks she can talk to me like I'm nothing more than trash. And what the *hell* does he want from me exactly? Because the thing is, I'm done wondering. I'm done with Jake Madsen.

I stand up and get right up in his face, because suddenly I am *furious*. "Clue in, Jake," I hiss. "You don't know me. You think you do, but you *don't*. You think you know what type of person I am, but you have no idea. And so, you don't get to do this. You don't get to interrupt my life over and over again and then think that I will be grateful to you for gracing my life with your very presence. After last night, I think it's perfectly clear that there is no reason for you to be here. So I am asking you again if we can have this conversation another time like *never*?"

I try to whirl around, but I'm caught up short because Jake grabs my hand and tugs gently. I have no choice but to whirl right back around to him and when I do, there is intensity in his eyes. He pulls me right up close to him and grinds out, mostly to himself, "It wasn't my intention to do this on a street corner, but this stubborn girl is gonna make me." Then he sighs and I'm staring at him with wide eyes because, frankly, what else can I do without making a huge scene. And did I mention that I'm tired?

He stares at me for a few beats, something softer coming into his expression before he continues, "You think I don't know you, Evie? I'll tell you what I know about you. That week I was following you, I know that you took the goddamn BUS to an old man's house to drop off cookies."

I'm momentarily stunned and I shake my head in confusion. "Mr. Cooper?" I furrow my brow. "He lived next to the house where I lived for four years. He was always nice to me. He's widowed. Lonely. He really likes my chocolate chip cookies."

"It's a two-hour round trip bus ride, Evie," he says gently.

I take a deep breath. "Jake, I'm sure there's a point here but—"

"That guy across the hall was going to kill me before he let me even think about so much as making you uncomfortable."

"Maurice?" I say, and now my face is all scrunched up because I am just plain confused. "He's a really protective guy."

"Like the guy last night who practically melted me with the angry lasers coming out of his eyes after he thought I disrespected you in public?" Jake asks, again gently.

"Landon?" I ask. "He's one of my best friends, he—"

"Evie, I think you're failing to grasp what I'm saying to you and so I'm going to spell it out for you here, baby."

Baby? Did he just call me baby? A thrill shoots down my spine, which I don't especially appreciate. *Don't let him charm you again, Evie.*

Jake's expression is still intense, but almost pained as he says, "You say 'please' and 'thank you' to everyone, Evie. You almost bumped into a cocker spaniel being walked by his owner and when you ducked around him, you said, 'excuse me.' You said 'excuse me' to a dog. And I bet you didn't even think twice about that. And that's because your manners are so deeply ingrained in you, that that is second nature. And given what I know about your past, I'm gonna guess that no one fucking taught you that. That is just all Evie."

I'm speechless, staring at him stunned, because I am just literally at a loss for words.

"What I *know* about you, is that people who are lucky enough to have your trust and your friendship, it is clear that they would have your back to within an inch of their life, and that is because you give them *you*, and they know that when they have you, they have a fuck of a lot.

"And, Evie, when you walk away from people, even strangers, you gotta know that their eyes follow you. And I'll tell you why, because I've felt it myself. It's because they don't want to see the light that is Evie, the light that is *you*, walking away from them. They want to see it coming *toward* them and staying *with* them."

"Uh—"

"So maybe I don't know what your favorite meal is, maybe I don't even know your birthday. But what I do know is *beautiful*, and Evie, what I do know lets me know that I want to know more."

He stops now and we stare into each other's eyes in the middle of the sidewalk, at a public bus stop, and for all I know, we're both standing on the moon.

"Um, Jake," I say.

"What, Evie?"

"I missed my bus. I'm gonna need a ride."

He looks at me for a minute and then his gorgeous face breaks into a big grin.

Oh, wow.

We don't say another word as he leads me to his car. He opens the passenger door and deposits me inside.

Jake walks around and slides into his seat, all smooth grace.

We pull out and Jake looks over at me and says, "I want you to listen to me about last night."

I bite the inside of my cheek, realize I'm doing it, stop and glance nervously over at him as he continues. So okay, he's charmed me again. But I'm still on alert.

"Gwen's father is the CFO of my father's company. And when I say 'my father's company,' I really mean to say 'my company,' because that's what it is now, but that's a transition my brain is still working on."

He's silent for a second. "Anyway, I've known Gwen and her father for a long time and over the years, Gwen and I have spent some time together here and there, although I always made it clear to her that I wasn't interested in anything more than what we had, and what we had was very little. Gwen made it clear that she was interested in more, and Gwen was raised to believe that she is entitled to what she wants and that eventually, if she whines enough, she'll get it.

"When I moved here, I tried to be a friend to her because, despite the fact that Gwen is a superficial bitch, I treated her disrespectfully over the years, and in part that was because a side benefit of screwing Gwen was screwing my father, who was embarrassed at my treatment of a colleague's daughter." He's silent for a second, frowning slightly, and I wonder what he's thinking, but I remain quiet.

"I had arranged the event last night with Gwen months ago, and I couldn't get out of it. It's a cause that is important to me, and I didn't think it was any real skin off my teeth to bring Gwen as I'd planned. Three seconds in and I realized that I was mistaken on that front, and that was even before I saw you there."

I don't want to feel satisfaction at this but I do. *God, I do*. But then I frown.

"Gwen made it sound like things were *very* current with you," I say, staring straight ahead.

"That's because Gwen saw the way I looked at you, she saw your beauty, and Gwen did what she thought would work to keep you away from me.

"I know that Gwen made you feel less-than because that is what Gwen does best, but, Evie, you could be wearing a gunny sack, rolling around in mud, and you would have more class in your little pinky than Gwen has in her whole designer-clad body. And Gwen knows that. And she hates that. And that is why she went out of her way to make you feel that way.

"It was killing me not to bust into that kitchen and pin you down and explain the situation to you, but you were working and I wasn't gonna make things worse for you."

I think back to what it felt like after Gwen walked out of that bathroom, how humiliated and hurt I was. I think about how Jake had made me proud of how hard I work to take care of myself, but in that moment, I felt full of shame not only for what I do, but also for who I am. And that searing shame is the same feeling that I lived with for most of my childhood. Then I look down at my Hilton uniform and my well-worn shoes, and I look around the luxurious inside of Jake's car.

"Jake," I start, "I might not be—"

But Jake pulls into a parking space in front of my building, turns off the car, and turns the full beauty of his face to me. "No, Evie. Whatever you're about to say, consider whether it goes in direct contrast to everything I've just said to you in the past half an hour and if it does, just throw it out, okay?" His expression is full of tenderness and my heart flips over.

I stare at him for a minute and then say, "Okay."

He grins at me again with those perfect teeth and says, "Good answer."

Then he's around the car, letting me out and he says, "I'm picking you up at six thirty tonight, and I'm making you dinner. Do you eat steak?"

"Yes," I whisper.

"Do you work tomorrow?"

"No, day off."

He walks me to my outside door and because I'm standing there staring at him, not moving, he takes my keys out of my hand and opens the door and then gives me a little push inside. Then as he's closing the door behind him, he says, "See you tonight. And, Evie, pack an overnight bag."

"What—" I sputter, but he's already gone.

CHAPTER THIRTEEN

I walk inside my apartment still spinning. How did this day take such a one-hundred-eighty-degree turn since this morning? How is it this man, in such a short period of time, has succeeded in taking complete charge of every situation? My nerves threaten, but I shut them down. I trust him. I *want* this.

I smile and hug myself after I've closed the door behind me. I sit down on the couch, biting my lip distractedly and thinking . . . I wasn't being gullible. My gut feeling told me to trust him and I wasn't wrong. Relief sweeps through me, not only because I like him, but because my own faith in my instincts about people is how I've survived so far. They're one of the most important things I possess . . . one of the *only* things I possess.

By six, I'm showered, shaved, and moisturized to within an inch of my life. I'm wearing my best jeans, a fitted, chocolate-brown sweater, with a deep V-neck that is tasteful, yet still shows plenty of cleavage and my high-heeled brown boots.

My hair is straightened and falling down my back, subtle makeup.

I've packed a small overnight bag with the essential bathroom items and a clean outfit to come home in tomorrow. But I had no idea what to pack to sleep in so I just threw in an extra pair of panties and the only decent nightie I own since I sleep mostly in T-shirts. I zipped it closed before I lost my nerve and took off to help fight the Mexican drug war, which sounded a whole lot less scary than spending the night with Jake Madsen.

Before I completely start melting down, I call Landon and as soon as he answers with "Fancy Face!" I blurt out, "I'm spending the night with Jake."

There's a beat of silence and then, "Whoa. Back up. Last episode, he had Catty Barbie hanging on him and you were wiping down her foot."

"I didn't wipe down her foot," I snap, "just her shoe. Anyway, you missed the episode where he picked me up after work, explained that she's the daughter of a business associate and they've messed around over the years, and now she wants him, but he has no interest in her, and he had the event with her planned months ago and couldn't get out of it. Oh, and he likes me, like really likes me and wants to get to know me better. And by better, I mean, whether I like dramas or action flicks, but also, like, pack your bag, you're spending the night with me, better."

"Wait," Landon says, "was that last night's recap of *Beverly Hills Housewives* or what happened with Jake since Friday night?"

"Very funny," I say. "You're not helping here, Lan. I'm freaking out. This is not my life. This stuff doesn't happen to me. Last Saturday night I was at home on my couch curled up with a good book and seriously thinking about getting a cat because I was kinda lonely. And maybe there was a really sweet kitty at the shelter who could use a good home, and could I afford to add possible vet bills to my budget? This was my thought process and my biggest concern last week, Landon."

"Okay, Fancy Face, slow down. You really are starting to concern me a little here. First off, you don't have to do anything that you're not ready for, okay?"

"Well, that's the thing, I think I *do* want this. That's the crazy part. I like him. He's sweet and thoughtful, but he's also intense and kind of bossy and he kind of freaks me out, but he makes me feel good, too. He makes me trust myself. He makes me feel special. And I, well, I think I want to give this a chance. Is that crazy?"

Landon is quiet for a second and then, "No, not crazy at all. Holy shit, my baby girl is growing up. He's a lucky son of a bitch. You know that, right, Fancy Face? And, babe, you *are* special."

"Thanks, Lan," I whisper.

"Okay, now let's get down to business. What panties are you wearing?"

"Um, red lace," I say. "Matching bra."

Nicole had given me two sets of sexy bra/panty combos on my twenty-first birthday, telling me that that was *my* year, and she had a feeling I was gonna need some amazing underwear. Turned out she was just a little off, but now I couldn't be more relieved I have something pretty to wear. Spending the night with Jake doesn't have to mean sex, but there *is* a chance Jake's gonna see my underwear tonight.

Oh God! Panic!

"Perfect. Where are you going?"

"He's cooking for me at his place."

"Cooking for you, huh? Sexy. Listen, Fancy, my best advice to you is to relax and let things play out. If you feel comfortable, you go with that, if you don't, you let him know and if he likes you like he says he does, he'll let you set the pace."

"Okay," I whisper. "You know I love you, right, Landon Beck?"

"I know, Fancy Face. How could you not? I'm very lovable."

I laugh and the doorbell rings.

"He's here! Gotta go. I'll call you tomorrow," I whisper.

"K, babe. If you don't, I'll hunt you down. Love you, too," he says back, and I quickly hang up.

I open the door and Jake smiles when he sees the overnight bag in my hand. And *God*, will I ever get used to how good-looking he is? He's just this big, strapping man and I want to do dirty things to him. And, holy smokes, it's like I don't even know myself anymore. *Cool it, Evie!*

He leads me out of my apartment, and when I see movement against Maurice's keyhole, I knock and say, "'Night Maurice." As Jake leads me to the front building door, I hear Maurice from behind his door say, "'Night, Evie."

He drives me to his condo downtown, telling me a little bit about his day, which sounds basically like meetings, meetings, and more meetings.

As we're driving, I wonder about something and ask, "Speaking of work, how'd you know when I was getting off work today?"

"I called the Hilton and told them I was picking you up and forgot what time you told me to be there," he says.

"Hmm, sneaky. I don't think they're actually supposed to give out that information."

"I'm very persuasive." He winks.

"Yeah, kinda getting that," I mutter.

We drive into an underground parking garage and he pulls into an assigned spot, then helps me out of the car, taking my small bag from me.

He uses a key card to open the door to a back stairway, and then leads me to a beautiful wood-paneled elevator, types in a simple code—I can't help noting it's 1-2-3-4, which doesn't seem like high security but it's not my business—and pushes the button for the top floor.

When we step out, there's only one door in front of the elevator, which means his condo takes up the whole upper floor. *Oh wow.*

He unlocks his door and leads me in, and I take in the huge open space in front of me. There are tall windows on every exposed wall, and I look out them at the beautiful city view. To our left is an obviously high-end, modern kitchen with black cabinets, black granite countertops and stainless steel appliances. The furniture is contemporary, all straight lines and minimal embellishment. The color scheme is mostly black and gray, with accents of white. It's all very stylish and sleek and obviously expensive, and I completely hate it. It feels cold.

Jake's looking at me and says, "Corporate condo. You don't like it."

Am I that easy to read? "No, no," I say. "It's really stylish. I was just thinking that it needs a little warmth. Maybe some colorful throw pillows or something." And oh my God, am I really giving him decorating advice? *Shut up, Evie.*

He smiles though. "I agree. I just don't know how long I'll be in this place. I'd like to buy something eventually."

He leads me farther inside and takes my jacket as I go to the window and look out at the city under a twilight sky.

I feel Jake's warmth before his body actually touches mine as he comes up behind me. He wraps his arms around me, pulling my back tight against his hard chest. For some reason, even though we've only known each other a short time, I feel completely comfortable with him. I melt back into his body.

We stand like this for several minutes, silently, me inhaling his delicious woodsy scent. I really need to find out the name of his cologne so I can find the creator and nominate him for some sort of Nobel Prize.

He lowers his head and sweeps my hair to the side, and I feel his lips on the back of my neck and shiver. "God, Evie," he whispers, "you feel so good. You smell so good. You undo me. And I haven't even had you yet. What will that do to me?"

I stiffen slightly. "Jake," I start, turning and bringing my arms up around his neck. I tilt my head back until I'm looking into his deep brown eyes. "About that," I whisper.

His eyes scan my face and he finally says, "You're nervous." It's not a question.

"Yes. No. I mean . . ." I shake my head and let out a shaky laugh.

"How about I make you dinner, we talk, hang out, and then if you want to sleep in the guest room, I'm okay with that tonight, all right? I'd like you in my bed. But I want it to be your call and if you're not ready, then you sleep in the guest room. I just want you here tonight, okay?"

"Okay," I whisper.

"Good," he says as his eyes move to my mouth just a second before he lowers his to mine. I feel him smiling as he takes my bottom lip gently between his teeth, slowly teasing me as he licks and sucks at my lips. My stomach dips, my legs weaken, and my body automatically melts into him even further.

He continues teasing me like this for several more seconds. He's driving me crazy and he knows it and finally, it's me who slides my tongue into his mouth. He moans deep in his throat, which completely ignites me. I slide one hand down his back and up his shirt. He's all hard muscle and smooth, warm skin and *God,* he feels so good.

Our kiss becomes rougher, our tongues tangling, mine intuitively dancing with his. I tilt my head and the kiss goes deeper, shooting sparks straight down my throat, into my belly, and ending between my legs.

I run my other hand up the back of his neck, cupping his head and sifting my fingers in his thick, silky hair.

I come back to reality as I feel the upraised, puckered skin of a scar underneath the softness of his hair, at the base of his skull. My fingers just start to trace it from behind his left ear to the middle of the back of his head when he tears his lips off mine, the heat from our kiss still in his eyes.

"What happened to you, Jake?" I ask. That felt like one hell of a scar.

He looks at me for a minute as if he's thinking about whether he's going to answer me or not. But then he says, "Remember the stupid shit I told you I did to earn my father's contempt?"

I nod, frowning.

The heat in his eyes has faded and now he's watching me closely as he says, "Some of that resulted in me tearing the back of my head open. Someday I'll tell you all about it, Evie, I promise. But how about right now I get dinner started?"

I frown and reach my hand up to his hair again and trace the scar. His eyes close, and he exhales before he reaches up and removes my hand and brings it to his lips to kiss it. "So damn sweet," he mutters.

Then he takes my hand, leads me to the kitchen, and sits me down on a barstool.

"Can I pour you a glass of wine and take a few minutes to change out of this suit?" he asks.

"How about you go change, and I'll open the wine and do the pouring?" I suggest.

"Perfect. The wine fridge is beneath the counter by the big fridge and the opener is in the drawer above it. Glasses are in that cabinet." He points to an upper cabinet made of glass and full of wine and champagne glasses.

"Got it."

He heads down a hallway between the front door and the kitchen, and I get to work on choosing a wine.

Ten minutes later when he re-enters the kitchen, he's in a pair of well-worn looking jeans and a black T-shirt. His feet are bare and his hair is damp. He must have taken a quick shower.

He grins at me, and I hand him his glass of wine. "Red," I say. "Hope that's okay. Goes with red meat and all."

This is the first time I've seen him in a T-shirt and I can see even more clearly how broad his shoulders are, how wide and muscled his chest is, and how his biceps flex when he takes his wine glass from me and extends it toward mine saying, "To beginnings."

I smile and clink my glass gently on his and take a sip, even though I've already been sipping mine as I waited at the bar.

He strides over to the fridge and removes a package of butcher's paper, and as he's opening it over the counter, he says, "Can I ask you a question? You told me the other night that you didn't date in high school. Why not?"

I'm sitting in Jake's kitchen, sipping wine while he cooks dinner for me. I feel protected and I feel relaxed, so I answer Jake honestly, even though I have never talked about my high school years to anyone, ever.

"When I was fifteen, my foster mom, Jodi, was diagnosed with cancer and she and her husband decided they couldn't foster anymore. I wasn't close to either of them, they were mostly disinterested in us girls who lived with them. They weren't unkind, just sort of indifferent and checked out. They watched a lot of TV and didn't take a big interest in getting to know who any of us were. We co-existed, and they mostly gave us what we needed physically, but emotionally, they were not parents to us, at least not in the way I define parenthood. But I was comfortable where I was. I liked the house, I liked the girls I lived with, and I thought life was as okay for me as it was gonna be in that situation.

"Anyway, when I was moved, I moved in with another couple and they made no bones about the fact that me and the other girls living there were drains on them, even though, as far as I could tell, the main reason we were there was for the checks we brought in. Me and Genevieve and Abby, the other girls who lived there, were mostly their slaves. We cooked, we cleaned, and we took care of their six-year-old twin boys who, it must be said, were good birth control for us girls if that was what they were trying to teach us. Our foster parents sat on their butts and if they wanted something, they hollered at us to run and fetch it for them. My foster mom, Carol, constantly made remarks about me, my body, my hair, my lack of personality, just being nasty. She was specifically mean to me, but she had an equal opportunity policy when it came to our care. She didn't spend one more cent than she had to on our needs, which meant that our clothes were constantly old and too small. At school, girls made fun of me because they thought I wore my clothes overly tight to get the boys to notice me. They called me a slut and worse, and the boys treated me like one and so I steered clear of everyone as much as possible."

I pause, the severe loneliness of that time enveloping me. I take a sip of wine before continuing. "I wasn't exactly brimming with self confidence as it was, but Carol made it her job to make me feel even worse about myself. This didn't exactly make me eager to put myself out there as far as making friends or dating. I ate my lunch in the library every day, and I went home after school and cleaned Carol and Billy's house. The day I turned eighteen, I got a job at the Hilton, and moved out with the intention of sleeping on Genevieve's couch for three months. She had moved out of our foster home and in with her boyfriend six months earlier and told me I could stay there until I had enough money saved up for a security deposit on an apartment. Two months into my stay, her boyfriend made a pass at me. Gen threw me out and I had nowhere to go, so I worked during the day, went to the library after work, and slept at a table in the corner for three hours until they closed. Then I wandered to several different coffee shops nursing coffees until it was time to go back to work, where thankfully, they have a shower in the employee restroom that they don't mind us using.

"I slept at a shelter downtown one night, but an old man tried to crawl into my cot with me in the middle of the night and someone stole the pair of shoes I had left at the end of my bed before I went to sleep. I couldn't risk someone stealing the money I had saved for an apartment, which I was carrying all in cash. I would have been right back where I started, and that was unthinkable."

I finally glance at Jake, and there's a hard look on his face, his jaw clenching. I go on anyway. It feels as if a dam has broken. I don't think I can stop myself now.

"At the end of that month, I had enough money for a security deposit at any one of the apartments I had looked at. I called around and found the one that I could move into that day. I slept on the floor using my backpack as a pillow and a ratty, pink blanket I had had since I was a kid, until I could afford some used furniture. I got my GED that next year since I had moved out and started working before I graduated."

He's still listening intently to me, and he takes my hand and squeezes it, giving me a small reassuring smile, although his face remains tense under it. There's something behind his eyes that looks like heartbreak.

While I've been talking, Jake has slowly been working, and now two seasoned steaks are in a pan on the stove and he's cutting several red potatoes into quarters that he's just rinsed in the sink on the counter in front of him.

"Want me to do that?" I ask, nodding toward the potatoes.

"No, I want you to sit there and relax and sip your wine and talk to me." He smiles now, his face relaxing.

"You've been through so much, Evie," he says, glancing up at me with sad eyes.

"Yeah, but the thing is, in some ways I'm lucky for it."

He frowns. "How so?"

"Well," I tilt my head, gathering my thoughts, "how many people do you think walk into their apartment at the end of the day, small and simple as it may be, and look around and feel like one of the luckiest people in the world? How many people truly appreciate what they have because they know what it feels like to have absolutely nothing? I went through a lot to get where I am and I don't take anything I have for granted, ever. That's my reward."

He's looking at me intensely, a fire in his eyes that almost looks like pride. I don't exactly understand it, but I appreciate it. Finally, he says quietly, "I never would have thought to look at it that way."

We're both silent for several minutes as he puts the potatoes in a bowl and pours in some olive oil and then opens a drawer and starts pulling out spices and tossing those in the bowl as well. Then he mixes it all with a spoon and pours the mixture on a baking sheet.

He turns to the stove, and as he's turning the dials and putting the baking sheet in the oven, I watch his back muscles flex under his T-shirt and check out his amazing ass, and wonder what it is about a man in jeans and bare feet that is just so damn sexy.

I take another sip of wine.

He takes a bagged Caesar salad out of the fridge and brings it back to the counter, winking and saying, "Not everything home made. Don't hold it against me."

I laugh. "Please. I'm already completely impressed."

"Reserve that until you've tasted everything." He grins and the mood seems to have lightened.

He turns the steaks over, and as he's mixing the salad in a bowl, he says, "Evie, the eulogy you gave for your friend, Willow. Tell me about that." He looks up at me and his eyes are sharp, focused.

"I'm talking too much about myself, again. How does that happen every time I'm with you?"

"Indulge me, you're fascinating to me."

I roll my eyes. That's me—*fascinating*. But I answer him anyway. "I used to tell Willow stories when we were kids and lived together in foster care. She loved them, and even after we were adults, and I would go over and clean her up from whatever mess she had gotten herself into: drug hangover, shit kicked out of her by a boyfriend, whatever." I wave my hand, trying to banish the images that immediately assault my brain. "Even as an adult she would ask me to tell her one of *her* stories. She would ask for them by name, even in a completely inebriated state sometimes."

Jake nods. "Sounds like she felt special in the ownership of them. She probably didn't have ownership of a lot. That's beautiful, Evie," he says gently.

I stare at him silently for a minute because that *is* beautiful when he puts it that way.

"In the beginning, it was just stupid kid stuff. I had a vivid imagination." I laugh a self-conscious laugh.

"It came in handy. Just a kid trying to comprehend the incomprehensible, you know?"

He nods as if he understands, which of course he doesn't but it's nice anyway. It's so hard to explain growing up in foster care to someone who has no concept of that type of childhood. Of course, Jake hasn't told me anything about his own childhood so I don't know what his upbringing was like. Obviously his family has money, though, so it was eons apart from mine, at least in that respect.

"Will you tell me about Leo?" he says.

I take a sip of my wine. "Jake, I've shared a lot tonight, and it felt good and that surprises me, because I don't make it a habit of bringing up my past very often, but can we save Leo for another time? Is that okay?"

I don't tell him that I'm struggling a little bit with the feeling I'm betraying Leo somehow, even though rationally I know that's ridiculous. He threw me away a long time ago, and he's not even of this earth anymore. I cringe inwardly with the thought.

He stares at me for a few seconds, and I start squirming at his intense gaze so I ask him what he's thinking.

He comes around the bar and sits on the stool next to me, and I turn toward him and he takes my hand and says, "I was just thinking about how much I appreciate you sharing with me tonight. And I was also thinking that from where I'm standing, you've done a pretty remarkable job of not letting your past make you hard. There's not a harsh or bitter thing about you, not a single thing, not your attitude, not the way you hold yourself, not your eyes, not your smile, not the way you treat people, always taking care of the people who are lucky enough to have your love, and that's just you. Life obviously took a lot from you, and I know you've been cut deep, but the fact that you relied on yourself to make it through and that you didn't let it make you cynical or cold, that is all you. Own that. That's what I was thinking."

A tear slips out of my eye. I can't help it. He's making slow circles with his thumb on my hand and staring at me with those soulful brown eyes. That's when I fall in love with him, just sitting in his kitchen; I fall head over heels. It's too soon and it's utterly ridiculous. But it's utterly true.

He smiles at me and gestures to the small glass table in the eating area next to the bar. I stand up and walk there as he pulls two placemats out of a drawer and puts them down on the table, and then places napkins and silverware for each of us.

I sit down, and he returns to the kitchen to dish up two plates and returns with them, and the bottle of wine.

He refills our glasses, and we dig into the food, which is completely delicious.

"Okay, truly impressed," I say. "This is amazing." And it is. The steak is tender and succulent and the potatoes are spiced perfectly with crispy skin on the outside, soft and fluffy on the inside. The salad is crisp and even though it's from a bag, it's the perfect compliment to the dinner Jake's made from scratch.

When we've eaten in silence for a few minutes, I say, "Will you tell me about your parents? How did your dad pass?" I glance at him, nervous that I've brought up a painful subject, but he answers quickly.

"Heart attack. It was sudden. He lingered for a week afterward but got a blood clot. That's what actually killed him."

"I'm sorry, Jake." I pause because his face seems like it's gotten hard. "You must miss him."

He sighs. "Yeah, I do. I wasted a lot of years with my dad that I can't ever get back."

"I'm sorry."

He smiles a small smile at me. "It's okay. Really. It wasn't okay for a long time, but I've come to a place where I'm getting there." He pauses for a minute before he continues. "I realize now that there are a lot of paths in life. Some we choose and some are chosen for us. I was dealt some shit, just like a lot of us are, and I made a lot of poor choices, too. I have to take responsibility for those. But the only thing we'll get from trying to figure out where another path would have taken us are questions there are no answers to, and heartbreak that can't be healed. Regardless of how we got there, all any of us can do is move forward from where we are."

He pauses and then says, "I'll tell you all about it, Evie. You've already given me so much of you, and I want to give you me, but not tonight. Tonight, I want to enjoy dinner and enjoy you and not bring up a bunch of shit that's going to put me in a bad mood. Okay?"

"Okay," I whisper, because it is. I feel like I know everything and nothing about Jake both at the same time and how can this be? I know how hard it is to share painful things with people, and that you have to feel ready to do that. No one should ever push you. I also know for sure that the man sitting in front of me is a *good* man. I grow more sure of it by the minute. The rest will come. Everyone has a past, right?

He grabs my hand and squeezes it, we finish our meal, and then I help him clear the table. I rinse the dishes and put them in the dishwasher as he drops the pans in the sink to soak.

I excuse myself to use his restroom, and when I come back, he takes my hand and leads me to the couch. He pulls me down on his lap so that I'm straddling him and then his eyes get lazy, and *God, that's beautiful.* I put my mouth on his because I can't stop myself. I lick the seam of his lips and he opens for me, and I'm the one to moan this time as he takes the back of my head in his hand and tilts it so that he can plunge his tongue in deep, and then we're kissing like we can't get enough of each other, like if a herd of zebras trampled through his living room right now, we wouldn't even come up for air.

A growl comes from deep in his throat, and a flood of wetness saturates the area between my legs. I grind down on his lap and he tears his mouth from mine.

"*Fuck!*" he clips and his eyes are fiery. "God, Evie, you feel so fucking good." He's breathing hard.

"Jake," I say, breathing hard too, "I'm not sleeping in the guest room tonight."

Relief fills his eyes and a breath whooshes from his mouth before he says, "Thank fucking Christ."

Then he stands up with me still in his arms, and I wrap my legs around his waist, and he carries me down the hall to his bedroom, kissing me the whole way.

CHAPTER FOURTEEN

Jake nudges his half-closed bedroom door open with his shoulder. Although the room is dim, I can see it's similarly decorated to the rest of the condo. There is a huge, and I mean *huge,* black four-poster bed against the far wall, two sleek, black dressers, and a set of white bedside tables flanking the bed. On the floor is a white, fluffy rug that looks like it's supposed to mimic an animal skin. The bedding looks like it's dark gray and white, although because of the low lighting, I can't be completely sure. The only light comes from what I'm assuming is the master bathroom.

Jake deposits me in the middle of his bed, and then stands up and removes his shirt. My mouth almost falls open at the sight of his bare, male beauty. I have a second to drink him in before he's back on the bed with me, and then his hands are up my sweater, my arms are forced up, and it's being pulled over my head. I hear it lightly hit the floor, and then Jake pulls back and is looking down at me, and even in the dim light, I can see his eyes are dark with something that looks like hunger. My heart jumps in my chest at the power of it. Sparks of both nerves and arousal are shooting through my body. *Is this really happening?*

"Help me out, Evie, I want to feel your skin on mine."

Yes, yes, I want to feel that, too.

And so I sit up slightly, unhook my bra and pull the straps down my arms and drop it on the floor. This is the first time a man has seen me naked, and I feel self-conscious for a second, but then the look of appreciation on Jake's face makes me relax.

He stares down at me for several long beats and then whispers, "Christ, even more beautiful than I imagined."

Then his mouth is on mine, his tongue in my mouth and his warm, hard chest against my breasts, and my hands are gliding over his back and his hips are rolling against me and *God, that feels amazing.* We both moan at the sensations.

And maybe I should slow this down because I'm a virgin, and I don't know if Jake figured that out after I told him about my nonexistent dating life or not. But I think I should probably make sure he's aware of that if this is going to go well.

He leans off me slightly as he kisses down my neck, and one of his hands comes up and cups my breast from underneath. His thumb rubs over my nipple, and I whimper, my hips bucking up and pressing into Jake's hardness. *Oh God, that feels good.* He growls low in his throat and then lowers his mouth to my nipple and sucks it into his mouth, and starts licking and sucking until I think I'm going to die with pleasure. He moves over to my other breast, and now my hands are in his hair and I'm moaning because I didn't know anything could feel so good, and I never, *ever* want him to stop.

I move one hand down his back again, and my other hand moves down to explore the warm skin over the defined muscles of his stomach, and he sucks in a breath, his mouth coming off my breast as he gazes at me. At the look of blatant lust on his face, I blurt out, "I'm a virgin."

He keeps gazing at me as heat moves up my face, and his eyes, impossibly, seem to warm even more. He's looking at me so intensely, and I feel self conscious, so I whisper, "Is that okay?"

He only pauses for a brief moment before murmuring, "In the history of the world, nothing has ever been more okay." His voice sounds deep and warm and slightly husky.

Then his mouth is back on mine—licking, sucking, nipping—and it feels greedy and demanding, and I *love* it. I feel his hand on the zipper of my jeans, and I lose his heat as he kneels up and takes my boots off, and then pulls my jeans and panties down my legs. He tosses them on the floor and then he's back over me, kissing me again, and I feel one of his hands slide down between my legs, and gently push them apart. I shiver. He brings his head up and whispers, "Open for me," and I do as he says.

"I'm gonna make it easier for you to take me," he says, and at his words I feel more wetness between my legs. *I want this. I want this so much.*

I feel one of his fingers press gently inside me, and I tremble at the invasion even though it feels incredible. Then his thumb hits *the* spot, and he begins moving it in slow circles, and my head tilts back and I moan deeply.

"God, you're so beautiful. Is that good?" he asks, his voice sounding strained.

"Yes," I pant out, and now he's added another finger, and he's moving them in and out of me as his thumb continues circling.

And it feels incredible.

My hips start lifting up to meet his hand, and he starts moving his thumb faster and harder, his fingers continuing their deep thrusting.

Yes, yes, *yes.*

"Oh my God," I pant. Jake moans.

I arch my head all the way back into the pillow, and for just a portion of a second, everything seems to freeze right before I tip over the edge and waves and waves of pleasure wash through me. I moan and cry out Jake's name, and when I open my eyes, several seconds later, he's crawling back over me, only now he's naked. *How'd I miss that?*

He leans over me and opens the nightstand drawer and pulls out a condom. I watch spellbound as he rips it open with his teeth, leans back on his heels and rolls it over his, *wow that's beautiful, too,* thick, hard shaft.

"Can I touch you, Jake? Will you show me how?" I whisper, wanting with everything in me to give him the same pleasure he's just given me.

"Next time, baby. Hanging on by a thread here. If you touch me, we'll both be sorry."

Then his weight is on me again, and he guides the tip of his erection to my entrance, and I automatically open my legs wider.

He kisses me again, his tongue thrusting slowly and deeply, hinting at what's to follow. I shiver with anticipation.

"Wrap your legs around me," he growls. "Gonna do this fast to get the painful part over with, okay?"

"Okay," I whisper, and just like that, he drives inside me in one smooth thrust, as I cry out, and the pain sears through me.

He's still for a minute, and then he starts to move slowly and the pain subsides until I just feel deliciously full and stretched. He keeps moving very slowly in and out of me until my body relaxes around him.

"Baby, I gotta move faster. You okay?" It almost sounds as if he's in pain.

"Yes," I whisper, and he starts thrusting in and out of me harder and faster, and watching the look of bliss on his face is the most beautiful thing I think I've ever seen in my life, because I'm giving that to him.

His mouth comes to mine again, and he starts thrusting his tongue into my mouth in time with the thrusting of his cock, and I like that.

Okay, no, I freaking *love* that.

I feel another fire building inside me as his pelvis presses into mine with every thrust, and as his breathing becomes ragged, I tip over the edge again, crying out. He drives deep, once, twice, and then again as he buries his face in the side of my neck and groans against me, circling his hips slowly as we both come down.

He lays still, buried inside me for a minute, and I hold him close to me, stroking my fingernails up and down his arms. He starts nuzzling my neck, and I feel his smile on my skin before his head comes up and his beautiful eyes are gazing into mine.

"You okay?" he whispers gently, smoothing a piece of hair away from my face.

No, no I'm not. I'm more than okay. *I'm fabulous.*

I gaze dreamily into Jake's eyes, his warm, hard body pressing against me. "Yeah," I whisper back, and I sound breathy.

He pulls out of me, and I mewl in protest at the loss, and that makes Jake grin. "My Evie likes me inside of her," he says.

I smile. *Yes, yes I do.*

"Let me get rid of this condom and get something to clean you up with. Stay there."

He sits up on the side of the bed, facing me and pulls on his boxers and T-shirt. Then he walks to the bathroom, and I hear some water running before he comes back out with a wet washcloth. He sits back down on the side of the bed and says gently, "Open your legs and bend your knees." I'm slightly embarrassed, but I trust him, and so I do as he says.

He cleans me with the warm cloth, and I notice there's blood. *Oh hell. How embarrassing.* But he doesn't make a big deal of it, which helps me feel a little less anxious.

Then he's padding back to the bathroom and I hear water again as I quickly find my panties on the floor and pull them on. Jake walks back in the room with a glass of water, which he offers me. I take long drinks and smile at him as I hand it back.

He puts the glass on the nightstand, and he climbs into bed next to me and pulls my back against his hard chest as he nuzzles his face into my hair.

I turn in his arms so that I'm facing him and look into his handsome face, running my hand down the side of his cheek.

"You're mine now, Evie. Say it," he whispers.

My hand stills, and I look him in the eyes. "I'm yours, Jake," I whisper back, loving the sound of the words.

I think I see a flash of something that looks like pain in his eyes and I feel a moment of confusion, but then he smiles that beautiful smile of his and kisses me gently.

"I've never experienced anything as beautiful as that," he says, and I feel my heart fill up because I feel the same way. I press myself closer to his warm body and learn something else that's beautiful about Jake Madsen. He's a cuddler.

CHAPTER FIFTEEN

Evie is Thirteen, Leo is Fourteen

I'm sitting on the sofa in the front room of my foster home, when there's a knock on the door. My foster mom, Jodi, calls from the back family room, "Evie, get the door!" and I stand up to answer it.

I note briefly that I'm wearing a really tight pair of jean shorts and a tank top with no bra, and so I open the door just a crack and lean my head out. Standing there is Willow and Leo. I swing the door wide open, saying, "Hey! What are you guys doing here?"

"Is it okay if we come in?" Leo says, and I notice his eyes sweep my body quickly, and he gets a tight look on his face. I realize I'm not really dressed to receive guests, but I didn't exactly expect any. I look at him questioningly, and he moves his eyes to Willow in a quick gesture, telling me all that I need to know.

"Of course," I say, waving them in.

"Who is it?" Jodi yells.

"A couple of friends," I yell back. "They won't stay long." There's no answer from the back room, meaning Jodi has gone back to whatever television drivel she's involved in right now. She won't bother us.

Leo sits down on the smaller loveseat, and I guide Willow over to the couch where I was sitting. I sit down right next to her and move her blonde hair out of her face. Her eyes are bloodshot and she smells like pot.

"Willow," I prompt when she just continues to stare straight ahead, "what's going on, baby girl?"

She continues to look straight ahead, but then her face crumples and she face-plants into my chest. I freeze for a second, but then I bring my hands up and stroke her hair, planting my lips on the top of her head and murmuring, "Shh, it's okay. Talk to me, Willow." I wait, but only get silence and the occasional sniffle.

"She showed up at my place stoned out of her mind," Leo says, his jaw clenching. "I had to sneak her away from there. My foster parents would have called the cops if they'd seen her. They're not exactly the easygoing types."

"Do you know what happened?"

"Yeah, she was mumbling about a court date. Her dad showed up and leered at her the entire time. Apparently he's expressing some interest in getting her back even though he hasn't given a shit about her for the last three years. That was all I really got out of her about that. Then some so-called friends snuck her out of her house and got her stoned and drunk and dropped her off to walk home. She showed up at my place. Nice fucking friends."

"Leo!" I hiss. "Don't swear." I cover Willow's ears.

He looks at me for several long seconds, and then his face breaks out into a grin.

I gape at him, shocked. "What are you grinning about?" I demand.

"You. You're so damn cute."

I snort. "Honestly, Leo? What is wrong with you? This is SERIOUS!"

He sobers his face and says, "I know, Evie, believe me, if I knew who her friends are, I'd go teach them a lesson about giving drugs to twelve year olds and letting them walk home alone."

I continue stroking Willow's hair until I notice she's snoring softly. I lay her back against the couch and grab the blanket on the end and cover her up with it. I watch her for a minute, chewing the inside of my mouth.

"Jodi's shows will be over in an hour. I'll need to get her out of here by then," I tell Leo.

He nods. "I think that'll be long enough for her to sleep some of it off. Come on over here and sit by me so we don't wake her."

I move over to the loveseat and sit down next to Leo, scooting as far as I can to the edge.

Leo gets a small frown on his face, but he doesn't say anything. He's been acting differently toward me lately, both in school and whenever we get together, which is usually at least once a week. It's confusing. He goes silent a lot and gets this strange look on his face. I can't tell if he's mad at me or what. He rarely tells me he loves me anymore like he used to. But then he makes comments about how cute I am. Boys are strange.

After a minute of silence, I bring my legs up to sit in the crisscross position and turn my body toward Leo. When I look at him, he's staring at my chest, but he quickly snaps his eyes to mine when he realizes I'm watching him. His cheeks get flushed.

Oh God! He's embarrassed for me because he realizes I totally need a bra. I'm not overly large, but I'm big enough now that going braless is unacceptable. He must be grossed out. My own cheeks flush, too, and I grab a pillow that's fallen to the floor and hug it to me, averting my eyes.

After a minute of awkward silence, Leo says, "I saw you talking to Max Hayes at lunch today." He sounds mad again. What is going on with him?

"Um, yeah, we have homeroom together. He's nice."

He doesn't say anything for a minute or two and then, "I heard that he kissed Zoe Lucas AND Kendall Barnes last week. I'd prefer it if you didn't talk to him at all. He's a player."

I laugh. "Leo, I'm not interested in kissing ANYONE, so relax, okay? You don't have to play this big brother role forever. I know you've protected me a lot in school over the years, and I appreciate that, but Max Hayes is not a threat to me."

He clenches his jaw again and moves his shaggy, dark blond hair out of his eyes and glares at me. "You wouldn't know a threat if it hit you between the eyes, Evie."

I narrow my eyes at him. Oh no, he didn't . . . really? And now I'm getting mad. "Oh, okay, LEO. I forgot that you're the worldly one and I've just been living in a protective glass case my whole life!" *I hiss, glancing nervously at Willow to make sure I haven't woken her. She lets out a snore and continues sleeping.*

Leo glares back at me. "That's not what I meant," *he says.* "You just don't know how guys work. You have no idea what Max is thinking when he's 'just talking' to you."

"Oh really?" *I say, leaning toward him.* "And how do you know what Max is thinking, exactly?" *I demand.*

"Because I'm thinking the same thing," *he hisses back.*

We stare at each other for several seconds before he closes his eyes and takes a deep breath, and then says quietly, "What I mean is, I'm thinking similar things about other girls, so . . . that's how I know."

I stare at him, a strange tight feeling expanding through my chest. I don't let myself think about it. Instead, I nod and look away, saying, "Thanks for the heads up. I'll make sure that I don't encourage Max, okay?"

He's silent for a minute before his eyes move from me over to Willow. "I think Willow's probably slept enough. I'll sneak her into her house."

We both stand too quickly, almost colliding, but he moves away first, going to Willow and shaking her slightly. She sits up, murmuring, "What's going on?"

Leo helps her up, saying, "Come on, Willow, you're gonna lean on me, and I'm gonna walk you home, okay?"

"Okay," *she says, sounding a little more with it.*

He guides her to the door, barely glances at me as I open it for them, and then calls out quietly over his shoulder as they walk down the stairs, "See you at school tomorrow."

I close the door behind them and stand leaning against it for a minute, wondering at why life always seems so painful and confusing, and wishing with all my heart I had someone to help me navigate it. After a few minutes, I sit back down on the couch alone.

CHAPTER SIXTEEN

I wake slowly in the early hours of morning and feel a warm, hard body against my back and smile as I remember the night before. I lay there for a quiet moment, reveling in the memory. I slowly move out from under Jake's arm and make my way to the master bath to do my business. After I'm done, I crawl back in next to Jake, snuggling into him again. I turn toward him this time and watch his beautiful face for a few minutes, his masculine jaw rough with morning stubble, his expression peaceful in sleep.

He cracks one eye open and smiles a sleepy smile at me. "Are you watching me sleep?" he asks, teasingly. "Who's the creeper now?"

I giggle and snuggle closer into his body heat. He wraps his arms around me.

We're still for a few minutes, and then I let my hand roam downward because his closeness has me buzzing again, and I need to feel him. He moans as my hand hits his crotch, and he's already hard so I rub him gently over his boxers, feeling him swell even more under my hand.

Suddenly I'm on my back, and he's over me. "You want to play, beautiful?"

"Yes," I whisper, nodding my head.

"Do you feel a little sore or are you okay?"

I squeeze my legs together, wincing slightly. Okay, so I am sore. "Just a little," I admit.

"Well, there are other things . . ." he trails off.

"Yes," I whisper again.

Then he's kissing down my belly, licking my navel with the tip of his tongue. He drags my panties down my legs and tosses them aside and then dips his head down to kiss the inside of my thigh. I shiver in arousal as he buries his head between my legs, and I automatically open to him. I feel him inhaling my scent, and he growls, "I love you smelling like me."

His soft tongue circles my already swollen clit, and my head presses harder into the pillow as I whimper.

Oh, *yes*.

Oh, *God!*

He begins licking and sucking gently, lapping at my swollen tissue with a steady, rhythmic suction until I feel my body quickening, and I cry out as the orgasm pulses through me.

Jake's tongue thrusts into my sex as I convulse, and I feel like I'm shattering into a million delicious pieces, my head thrashing back and forth on the pillow as I chant his name again and again.

He crawls back up the bed, kisses the side of my neck and then collapses next to me, pulling me into him, and my hand goes under the bottom of his T-shirt to trace the ridges and dips of his stomach muscles.

And now it's my turn to explore.

I lean up and just like he removed my sweater last night, I scoot his shirt up his waist, and then he reaches his arms up, sits up slightly as I pull it over his head, and toss it on the floor.

He's looking at me with that beautiful, lazy look, and his hair is messy from sleep. His beautiful, hard-muscled chest is on display, and for a minute all I can do is stare at him and drink in his perfection. Is he real? Is THIS real? My tummy clenches with the thrill of being in this bed with *this* beautiful man as we explore each other's body.

Then I lean over and put my mouth on his chest, kissing, tasting and licking my way down until I get to one hard nipple. I lick it and suck the tiny bud into my mouth like he did to mine last night. He groans, and I smile against his chest, loving that I'm bringing him pleasure.

My hand wanders back down his stomach, and I lift my head to look at him.

"Teach me what you like," I whisper.

"Just put your hand on me. I just want you to touch me."

He leans up slightly and pulls his boxers down, and I watch as his stomach muscles clench beautifully and his big, hard cock springs free. Then he kicks the boxers off his feet to land on the floor next to the bed.

I lean up on one elbow and scoot down a little bit so that I can reach him, and when I wrap my hand around his rock-hard length, it jumps slightly in my hand.

There's a small, wet drop at the tip of his shaft, and so I take my thumb and rub it in slow circles to which he groans.

"Move your hand up and down, baby," he chokes out. "Like this," and then he puts his hand over mine and shows me. And the sight of his hand over mine on his impressive erection sends little sparks between my legs even though I just had an orgasm less than five minutes ago.

I begin moving my hand, slowly at first and then faster, learning what he likes and responding to his breathing and his moans.

As my strokes become faster, I feel his cock jump and swell in my hand. He chokes out, "Evie!" as white cum spurts over my hand.

"Oh *Godddd*!" he moans as he comes down, my hand slowing.

I keep watching his cock as it slackens in my hand, and then I look up at him, not able to contain the huge, proud grin. And it's ridiculous because it's not as if I've just performed brain surgery, but there's something utterly thrilling about giving Jake an orgasm, and I can't help feeling completely satisfied with myself.

I keep grinning my proud grin at him, and he bursts out laughing and then reaches under my arms and hauls me up so that I'm lying on top of him and he's looking in my eyes. "You're a natural," he says grinning back at me.

I lay my head on his shoulder and nuzzle into his neck, and we lay like this for long minutes until Jake says, "I'm gonna run a bath for you while I make breakfast. Then you're gonna spend the day with me."

"Hmm . . . bossy," I mutter, but I smile against his neck. I want nothing more than to spend the day with him.

I stand up and start walking to the bathroom, and when I glance behind me, shooting Jake a flirty look, he's looking at my naked backside with a look of appreciation on his face as he's pulling his T-shirt and boxers back on, covering that gorgeous body. It's surprising to me that big, beautiful, perfect Jake Madsen seems to be a bit modest.

CHAPTER SEVENTEEN

I soak in Jake's Jacuzzi until my skin is pruney and my body is flushed all over, then I dry off with one of his thick, luxurious towels and moisturize my skin with the lotion in my overnight bag Jake brought into the bathroom for me.

I pull on my clothes: a pair of black, skinny jeans and a white, long-sleeved, V-necked shirt with a gray sweater. I packed a pair of black, canvas sneakers, but I stay barefoot for now.

I do light makeup and pull my hair back into a low, messy bun, then follow the delicious smells of coffee and bacon into the kitchen.

Jake's standing at the stove, but looks back over his shoulder as he hears me enter the room, shooting me a smile. "Omelet?" he asks, using a pair of tongs to remove bacon from a frying pan on the stove. He places the strips on a plate covered with paper towel, and sets it on the counter next to a plate of cut-up cantaloupe.

I shake my head no. "Just coffee and fruit is plenty for me."

"Okay, help yourself to coffee. Cups are above the coffee maker. Milk in the fridge, sugar on the counter."

He turns back to the stove and cracks a couple eggs into a pan as I go about getting myself a cup of coffee, no sugar, and a generous amount of milk.

I sit at the counter sipping my coffee and admiring Jake's ass until he pours his omelet on a plate and joins me, adding bacon and fruit to his plate.

"I have cereal, too, if you'd prefer that."

"No, really, this is perfect. I usually don't eat much in the morning."

"Well, babe, things have changed for you. You're gonna have to keep up your energy now." He winks, trying to contain the teasing smirk and looking extremely pleased with himself.

I pick up a skinny piece of cantaloupe. "Oh, right. This should do the job," I say, eating the fruit in two small bites and discarding the rind on the napkin in front of me.

He bursts out laughing, stands up, and scoops me up planting me on his lap on the bar stool, straddling him. He nips at my neck and tickles my sides, making me squeal and giggle. "I can see I have more to prove to you, minx." Then he's nipping at my ear and growling as his hands roam over me, and I can barely catch my breath I'm laughing so hard. Minx? Really? Who says that?

"Okay! Okay! No more. Seriously, Jake." I squirm into him, and it's not lost on me that he feels good . . . *really good.*

He's laughing, too, obviously teasing, but he growls one more time for show. "I can see it's sinking in for my girl now how much she's gonna need a good breakfast."

I press into him, rolling my hips, turned on again. "Okay, seriously, speaking of sinking in," I say, licking the dip at the base of his neck and kissing up to his jaw.

He groans. "Evie, I thought you said you were sore."

I sigh, sitting up. "I am. Maybe some Tylenol would take the edge off enough?"

He bursts out laughing again. "Christ. I've brought a sex demon to life."

I laugh, climbing off him, but he might be right. "Okay, so then. What are you going to do with me today?"

"Ever been to the zoo?" he asks.

"Actually, no," I say, surprised. "You're gonna take me to the zoo?" I grin thinking that sounds fun. I never got to do any of that kind of stuff as a kid and so I suppose there's a lot I've missed out on. And I don't exactly have the extra cash to spend on weekend outings now.

"Cool. Do you have shoes that'll work for walking?"

"Yeah, I brought a pair of sneakers."

"Okay, good. I'll take a quick shower and we'll get going."

I nod. *Wet Jake. I'd like to watch that. Yum.*

He finishes his breakfast quickly as I enjoy my coffee, and then he drops his dishes in the sink, kisses me on the cheek, and heads to the shower.

A minute or two later, I get the naughty idea to surprise him, but when I try the door, it's locked. I frown slightly. *Okay . . .*

I head back to the kitchen and instead wash the pans from last night's dinner and breakfast, and load the dishwasher. As I'm finishing up, Jake enters the kitchen in a pair of jeans and a black pullover. His beautiful caramel hair is perfectly tousled and still a little damp. I go to him and put my arms around his waist, inhaling his delicious, fresh woodsy scent, laying my head on his chest for a minute. It seems impossible that I missed him for the ten minutes he was showering, but I can't deny it, I did. I lift my head and grin up at his masculine beauty, and he's smiling down at me. He leans and kisses me on my forehead, whispering, "My Evie. So sweet," before pulling away and going to put on his shoes.

****

It's probably one of the best days of my life. It's a beautiful, crisp fall day, slightly cool, but with lots of sunshine to take the worst of the chill off. Jake and I hold hands as we walk through the zoo, laughing and chatting easily. I'm seriously fascinated by some of the animals and watch them for long minutes before looking over at Jake who seems to always be looking back at me with a grin. He seems to enjoy my reactions as much as I'm enjoying the experience.

We stop for hot dogs and ice cream for lunch and as we're sitting there eating, a peacock walks right by us. Apparently, they freely roam the zoo. I gasp and pick up my phone, trying to get a picture, following the bird around like a crazed prom mom. Jake's laughing at me from the table as I dance around like a nut, trying to get a shot, when suddenly the bird saunters right over, halts in front of me, and spreads his feathers in a show of beauty like I've never seen before. I'm frozen as I stare, spellbound by this beautiful creature. He prances in front of me for several seconds before I unfreeze and snap picture after picture, cooing to the beautiful boy before he preens off for greener pastures.

I suck in an excited breath as I hurry back to Jake. He's sitting at the table with a little frown on his face. "Look!" I squeal, showing him the pictures of the gorgeous bird that clearly wanted to show off for me. He makes little "big deal" grunts as I'm scrolling through the pictures, and so I glance at him quickly, noting his expression. "You're jealous of a bird?" I ask incredulously.

"What?" he says. "No." But I can tell he's lying.

"You're jealous of a bird," I say. It's not a question. I look back at the pictures. "He IS gorgeous. Goddddd, soooo gorgeous," I say, moaning out the syllables in an exaggerated way and throwing my head back.

"Hilarious," he says. But I can see that despite himself, he's laughing.

"That bird was trying to move in on my territory," he says deadpan. "I know a brazen male threat when I see one."

I laugh out loud at him, and he's trying not to laugh, too, but he loses in the end as he grins at me, showing those perfect, white teeth.

"You're ridiculous," I say. But I sit down on his lap and grab his gorgeous face in my hands, and we're both smiling. But then we're both serious, and he's staring at my lips and I can feel him swelling under my ass.

"Jake—" I start.

"Evie—" he finishes.

Then I'm kissing him, hot and wet, right in the middle of the zoo, as our ice cream melts.

I pull away and rest my forehead to his. "I had a really, really nice day, Jake."

"It's not over yet, baby," he says, taking my hand and pulling me up off his lap. "Let's go see the tigers."

****

We leave the zoo at almost five o'clock, thoroughly exhausted. As he pulls out of the gate, I look over at Jake, feeling happy and sleepy. He grabs my hand and holds it as he drives with his left. We drive in silence, listening to the radio, and I close my eyes a few times, feeling completely safe and at peace in the warmth of his car.

He pulls into a parking lot, and I note that it's a small, Italian restaurant. He comes over and opens my door and helps me out. He leads me into the restaurant, and I look around, noting that it's quaint and adorable, almost full even early on a Sunday night.

The hostess rushes up to us and with a warm smile leads us to a small table in the back. Once we're seated, the waiter comes up to our table quickly and Jake orders a bottle of red, which the waiter is back with before I've even read down two items on the menu.

"The eggplant parmesan is really good," Jake offers and so I close my menu and raise my glass to his. "To hot peacocks!" I say, grinning.

"Hmmph," he snorts, teasing, then grinning at me and clicking my glass. *God, he's so adorable.*

We order dinner and chat easily as we're waiting for the food, holding hands across the table.

"What shift do you work tomorrow?" Jake asks me.

"Ten to seven all week."

He looks at me thoughtfully for a minute and then asks, "Ever think about doing anything else?"

"You mean do I have ambitions to be more than a maid?"

"Yeah. I mean, you know I don't think there's anything wrong with what you do. You're just so smart, you could do anything. I was just wondering if you think about it."

I sigh. "Yeah, I do, actually. I'd love to go to college, but that takes money. Money that right now, I don't have. But what I'd really love to do is write. I have this idea for a book . . ." I trail off, feeling slightly embarrassed.

"Do it. Why haven't you?"

Because it's out of my realm of "safe."

"Well, I need a computer to be able to write. I brought a flash drive back and forth to the library for a while, but it's just too impractical. And when I was feeling inspired, the library was closed . . . you know. It just didn't work."

The waiter brings our dinner and we dig in. It's rich and delicious and I can't help moaning after I take the first bite.

"Good?" Jake asks, his eyes darkening as he watches my mouth.

"Mmm," I say, nodding.

"Will you stay with me again tonight?"

"I can't, Jake. I need to get ready for the week. I need to go home and get myself organized."

"Tomorrow night?"

"Can't tomorrow night either. I have a catering job that'll go late. I don't usually do them on Monday nights, but it's some sort of art showing at a gallery downtown." I look at him suspiciously. "You won't be there, will you?"

He grins. "Wasn't planning on it, but maybe now I'll have to see what I can arrange."

"Don't you dare."

"I have to travel to my office in San Diego on Tuesday, but I'll be back Wednesday evening. Will you stay then?"

I smile at him. "Okay." He smiles back.

We eat in silence for a minute, and then I ask, "I'm assuming you went to college?"

"Yeah, I went to UCSD. I was in school and also working with my dad, learning all about the company since the plan was for me to start working there when I graduated. We just had no idea at the time that I'd be running the damn thing. That's when my dad and I finally formed more of a relationship than we'd ever had. I had moved out of our house, and that was really the thing that allowed us to start over. It was the first time I was really something close to happy in a long time, being away from my parents, just 'finding myself' to use a clichéd expression."

I nod. "You're not close to your mother?"

He makes a scoffing sound. "Close?" He cringes and is silent for a few seconds. "No."

I keep looking at him, but he doesn't go on and I don't know what to say, so I pick up my fork and continue eating.

After a minute, he says quietly, "I want to pay for you to take classes, Evie."

I blink at him. "What?" I bristle slightly. "Why would you do that?"

"Because I believe in you. Because I think you're smart, and I think you just need a small break to be able to reach for your dreams."

I shake my head slightly. "Jake, listen, that's a nice offer, but I've worked really hard to get where I am. I know to you my life probably doesn't look like a raving success story, but I do okay, and I'll find a way to go to school at some point. I mean we just started sleeping together, and I don't really know how all this works, but maybe we should wait to see where this goes before you start offering me large sums of money."

His face is hard now, clearly not happy with what I've just said. "First of all, I thought I already made it clear that, actually, I do consider your life a raving success story, all things considered. And secondly, do I need to remind you what you told me in my bed not twenty-four hours ago, Evie?" *Yikes. He's pissed.*

I blink again because I said a lot of things, most of them having to do with my approval of what he was doing with his hands and his mouth and . . . *God, now I'm turned on again.*

"Um—"

"You told me you were mine, Evie. This is not some fun fuck. This is not casual to me. I thought I had conveyed that to you."

"So, what? You're like my boyfriend or something now?"

"Boyfriend, man, lover, whatever label you like, you can use it, but what it means is that we take care of each other in and out of the bedroom. And part of me taking care of you means me offering to give you the money it takes to make your dreams come true."

Oh wow. Okay, then. It's bossy, but I can't help the warmth that spreads through me at the intensity of Jake's words. Someone wants to protect me, care for me . . . something I've had so little of in my life. "Jake—"

"Just think about it, okay?"

I stare at him for a second, but relent, "Okay."

"Okay." He takes a couple bites of his dinner and then, "Also, you need to get on birth control. I don't want to use condoms with you."

I pause, a bite halfway to my mouth. *All righty.* "I'm already on the pill. I have bad periods. It regulates it. I've been on it for years."

He stares at me silently for a second and then, "Okay, good. Now finish your dinner."

Totally bossy. But totally sweet. And totally hot. But . . .

"Um, Jake, if we're not going to use condoms, I should probably ask—"

"I'm clean. I've always used condoms and I get regular check ups. I can show you paperwork if you want." He looks down and something that looks like shame passes over his expression.

It's not his look of shame that causes me to trust him. It's just him. The whole package. I need him to know that. So, I lean across the table and take his hand in mine. I'm silent for a second, then say, "No, I trust you."

After dinner, Jake drives me back to my apartment, and we make out in his car for a few minutes, but then he groans and pulls away, muttering, "*Killing me,*" and comes around the car to open my door for me. I give him one last kiss, open my building door, and practically skip inside.

CHAPTER EIGHTEEN

Evie is Thirteen, Leo is Fifteen

I heft my backpack up on my shoulder as I walk down the street toward Leo's foster home. I stayed late for a study group and so I'm not walking with Willow like I usually do.

Leo started high school several months ago, and not having him at the same school anymore has been hard. He hasn't had to stand up for me for a while. Kids started ignoring me after the Denny Powell incident, but just seeing him in the halls would brighten my day. Sometimes he would reach out and brush his hand against mine, pretending not to see me as we passed in the hall, or he would leave funny little notes in my locker. It made me smile. And I can use all the smiles I can get.

As I turn the corner to his house, I see a lone, familiar figure sitting on his porch stairs. I stop and stare at him for a minute, knowing he doesn't see me, apparently lost in thought, his elbows on his knees, his head bent forward.

I head in his direction, and as I walk toward him, his head comes up and he looks up at me, his face breaking out in a smile.

"Hi," I say, smiling back. "What are you doing out here?"

"Just thinking," he says, looking more serious now. "It's so damn loud in there." He gestures backward with his head.

I take a seat next to him, nodding. "Whatcha thinkin' about?"

"I was thinking about Seth." He pauses. "I was wondering where he is, how he's doing . . . wondering . . ." *His voice breaks, and I instinctively reach out for his hand, bringing it to my cheek, rubbing his knuckles against my skin.*

His eyes dart to me and his lips part slightly. My eyes go to his mouth, and I stare for a minute, wondering what it would be like to kiss him.

Oh my God! Did I just wonder what it would be like to kiss Leo? He's always been like a brother to me. But lately . . . I think about him in ways I never have before. I find myself wanting him to hold my hand, to sit close to me when we watch television together at my house in the front room. I shiver when he accidentally brushes against me.

I love him. I already know that. I've loved Leo McKenna for so many years . . . but am I falling IN love with him?

When my eyes meet his, there's an intensity there I've seen before, but never knew what it meant. I know now. I probably have the same look in my eyes, too. A single thought pops into my head, "Kiss me!"

"Wanna walk?" *he asks.*

I let go of his hand and stand up. "Sure."

We walk together in silence for a couple minutes, and then he takes my hand and looks shyly at me. I smile at him as warmth seems to spread from our joined hands, up my arm to spread through my chest. He smiles back and squeezes my hand tighter.

We turn into the park and walk to the swings. I sit down on one and he pulls it back and lets it go so that I giggle. He leans against the support pole a few feet away.

Leo grins, showing me that adorable gap and says, "I love to hear you laugh."

I tilt my head as my swing slows. "You do?"

He comes closer until he's holding both chains on my swing, and I have to tilt my head to look up at him. "Yeah, Evie, I do. It's the only thing that makes me truly happy."

We both grow serious as he gazes down at me, and I feel like my heart dips into my stomach. But then he moves back slightly and stuffs his hands into his pockets. I blink and swallow nervously.

"I was wondering . . . I know it's a girl ask boy thing. But, well, I wanted to know if you'd go to that Sadie Hawkins dance at my school with me." His cheeks flush slightly as he waits for my answer.

"I'd love to go to the dance with you, Leo. Only, I don't exactly have anything to wear. It's not like Jodi will buy me anything for something like that." I look down and my cheeks heat, too.

He nods, looking at me thoughtfully, probably realizing he didn't think about the fact we'd need dress-up clothes. "Then we'll say we're going to the dance, and instead we'll come here and dance under the stars. No dressing up required for that. Our foster parents will never even notice that we're not dressed right for a dance." He smiles a little sadly at me, but I know he's right about that. But then his smile widens. "I just want to be with you. I want to hold you close."

"Where will we get music?" I ask quietly.

"I'll bring my handheld radio." He grins.

I can't help but to grin back. "We'll probably get arrested and spend the night in juvi."

"I'll risk it."

I tilt my head to the side. "Okay. It's a date." I smile hesitantly as he grins back at me.

He stares at me for a few seconds and then says very seriously, "Someday, I'm going to buy you a whole closetful of the most beautiful clothes money can buy."

I smile up at him. "I don't need fancy clothes, Leo. I just need you."

"You can have both," he says smiling back.

I stare at this boy, my Leo. How did things change so quickly? Did I fall for him so slowly that I didn't even notice while I was falling? As he grabs my hand and pulls me off the swing and we start walking back, my heart starts beating wildly in my chest. I think dazedly that falling, whether to the ground or in love, is always at least a little bit scary, even if you do it slowly.

CHAPTER NINETEEN

The next couple of days go by quickly in a flurry of work, laundry, and other mundane, but necessary activities.

Jake offers to drive me, or have his company driver chauffeur me to and from work, but I tell him no. I don't mind taking the bus. I can read while I'm riding and it's convenient for me. He doesn't seem particularly pleased about this, but I need to maintain my independence. I already feel like things are moving so fast between us, and it scares me to become so wrapped up in someone so quickly. What if he goes away? What if this all ends?

I talk to Jake on Monday between my two jobs, but he's at work and he sounds distracted, so I make it quick and tell him I'll call him on Tuesday night while he's in San Diego. He has a smile in his voice as he says he'll be waiting for my call.

On Monday night I work for Tina at a small art gallery downtown and Landon is there, too, so, between filling trays in the kitchen, I fill him in on my day and night with Jake. He hangs on my every word and fans himself dramatically as I throw in a few tidbits about our night together.

"Down, boy. That's all you're getting. A girl's got to keep a few secrets," I say teasingly when Landon asks for more details.

"No fair, I've been waiting a *very* long time for this," Landon grumps back.

I smack him lightly on the shoulder, "You act like I was the last virgin known to mankind."

"Not the last known to mankind, but possibly the last one over twenty-one. Have you looked around our society lately, Fancy Face? I was just dying to know who exactly you were saving yourself for." He winks and grins at me.

"I wasn't saving myself. You could have had me anytime," I say back bumping my hip to his playfully.

"That's it. I officially renounce my gay-ness. I'm yours, Fancy Face. Take me now!"

"Ha ha. Don't think it works that way, Lan, but I appreciate the sentiment." I grin at him and get back to work.

But later I think about what Landon said about saving myself. Had I been? Because deep down, I realize that maybe me denying it wasn't entirely true. I had made a promise a long time ago and although that person was no longer a part of my life, nor was he ever going to be, somewhere inside I always knew if I was going to fall in love again, it was going to be because something in that man reminded me of Leo.

****

On Tuesday evening, I make a couple batches of chocolate chip cookies, dropping one off to Mrs. Jenner and one off to Maurice. I chat for a few minutes with both of them and then make my way to the bus stop, off to see Mr. Cooper. He's sitting on his porch as usual, waiting for me when I walk up, smiling and greeting me with a big hug.

"Evelyn," he says, gesturing for me to take my usual seat on the porch swing as he sits down in a cushioned chair. It's a crisp evening, so he offers me an afghan to lie over my legs, and I keep my coat on. He has a blanket over his legs as well.

"How are you?" I ask, smiling, placing the cookies down on the small table next to the porch swing and taking the foil off the plate.

He smiles warmly. "Couldn't be better. Got a pretty girl to visit with and a plate of homemade cookies."

"Take one." I gesture toward the plate and he grabs a cookie. I follow suit.

After a minute he says, "And what's new with you, Miss Evelyn?"

I finish chewing before I respond, feeling a little shy. "I'm dating someone," I say quietly.

He looks surprised for a second, probably because I've never mentioned a boyfriend in all the years I've known him. But then he smiles widely. "And who is the lucky gentleman?"

"His name is Jake. He runs a company that does something with X-ray technology." I wave my hand indicating I'm not real clear on what exactly that is. "He's . . . nice, and smart and handsome and . . ." I blush, looking down and feeling awkward suddenly.

But Mr. Cooper is still smiling, watching me closely. "Why, Evelyn, I do believe you're in love."

"Oh!" I shake my head quickly. "No, it hasn't been long at all. I practically just met him."

He studies me for a second and smiles tenderly. "Knew the first time I laid eyes on my Mary that she was the one for me. Didn't doubt it for even one second for the next forty-three years."

I look at him sadly, my heart squeezing. I know the loss of his late wife is still a tender subject for him, even though it's been many years since he lost her.

"Does he know what he has in you, Evelyn?"

I'm not sure what he means exactly, but I answer, "He seems to really like me, too. He makes me feel . . . special . . . wanted." I blush again. It's kinda weird to talk about my love life with someone whom I consider a grandfather figure.

"Good. You *are* special. I knew it the first time I saw you out in that yard, playing so patiently with those two little demons." He laughs. "Then later, sitting alone on the porch, looking so sad, but always holding your head high. I knew you were hurting, but that you were brave."

I look down, remembering those days. "I was never brave, Mr.

Cooper. I was scared all the time as a kid, and then as a teenager, too. All the time." I end on a whisper.

"I know that, Evelyn. But it didn't keep you from showing kindness to everyone I ever saw you with, including me. It didn't keep you from sitting with an old man on his porch just to chat for a minute or two because you saw I could use a smiling face. It didn't keep you from bringing out a glass of water when you saw me mowing my lawn in the summertime. Even now, you think I don't know that it's hard for you to come near that house," he gestures to my old foster home, "or how long it takes you to bring me a plate of cookies?"

I look up at him. "I love bringing you cookies, Mr. Cooper. I get to visit with you."

"See what I mean?" He smiles.

I look down again, studying my nails, embarrassed. He continues, "You know why I call you Evelyn, instead of Evie like everyone else does?" he asks.

I shake my head no. I just thought he liked it because he's from a more formal generation and liked using my full name, rather than a casual nickname.

He's quiet for a second, obviously gathering his thoughts. "I don't want to bring anything too personal up, Evelyn, because we've never talked about the circumstances that brought you to that foster home next door all those years ago. But I know that I can't say much for your mama, leaving you there, never coming back. I reckon you probably don't have a lot to say for her either."

I remain quiet. He's right about that.

"But your mama, she did at least two things right. She gave you life, and she gave you a name fit for a lady. And that, Evelyn, is exactly what you are—a lady, through and through. You make sure that gentleman friend realizes it." He smiles then and I blink back tears.

I tilt my head to the side and say, "Since we're on the subject of compliments, I have something I'd like to share with you, too." I smile.

"Okay." He smiles back.

I pause for a minute as I grow serious and say, "I never had a whole lot of love in my life. Many times, I had a whole lot of just the opposite. But everywhere I went, I seemed to find at least one person who gave me kindness and made me feel special. When I lived here," I gesture to the house next door, "that person was you. You gave that to me and you have no idea what it meant. Thank you."

Mr. Cooper wipes at a tear in his eye, saying, "Gettin' soft in my old age, huh?" But he laughs and smiles at me with that same kindness he's always shown me.

"So," he says, obviously changing the subject, "guess who was running around the yard in her unmentionables a couple days ago after her dog snatched her wig and took off out the door?"

I almost choke on a bite of cookie as I laugh out, "What?"

I know exactly who he's talking about. My ex-foster mother, Carol, always wore a wig and swore no one could tell, even though it always looked like she had a dead beaver on her head. I used to wonder what horror lay beneath if she thought *that* looked better than what she was hiding.

Years ago, my ex-foster father had moved out with their boys, the twin demons. Apparently he'd had enough of his witch of a wife, and I couldn't say I blamed him. I got the hell out of there the minute I was able to, too. What took him so long, I didn't know.

"Yeah, me, the mailman, and half the block stood around laughing our butts off, not lifting a finger to help her and not feeling badly about it." I wasn't surprised. She'd been nasty to everyone who crossed her path for years.

"That mangy mutt thought it was a game and just ran faster. Not that it was probably very hard to dodge her. She's gained about two hundred pounds since you moved out, and she had about that much to *lose* when you lived here."

I can't help it. I'm laughing so hard I have to clutch my stomach even though I know it's mean. "What was under there?" I finally ask, eyes wide.

"Oh, Evie, darlin', wouldn't burden you with the description. I'm still rinsing my eyes out with acid nightly to try to burn the image from my retinas." Now we're both laughing.

We visit for a while longer, and when it's time for me to go, Mr. Cooper takes my hand and kisses it. "Lady Evelyn," he says, smiling. "Until next time. You be safe."

I give him another big hug and walk down his steps, smiling as I walk away.

****

When I get home, I take a shower and change into a pair of PJs. I brush my teeth, and then I climb into bed, pulling my phone out and dialing Jake's number. I smile slightly as I anticipate his voice picking up. Instead, I'm surprised when a woman answers his phone, so surprised that I'm silent for a second as she repeats, "Hello?"

"Um, hi," I stammer. "Is Jake there?" I furrow my brow, a lump forming in my throat.

"He's in the shower," she clips out, clearly irritated. "Who is this?"

"Uh, no message. I'll call him back later." I hang up quickly.

What the hell?

I sink back onto my pillows, a feeling of emptiness washing through me. *There's a woman in his hotel room while he's showering?* I don't know what to think or what to do. Should I call back in half an hour? Or should I just leave it?

Finally, I turn off the light and attempt to fall asleep. I toss and turn for hours, but Jake never calls.

LEO (A SIGN OF LOVE NOVEL)

****

In the morning, the ringing of my cell phone wakes me. I open my eyes slowly, groggy and disoriented. I didn't fall asleep until well after one o'clock and it's only six o'clock now.

"Hello," I mumble into my phone.

"Evie." It's Jake.

I pause. "Hey," I say, coming more awake.

"Hey, you never called me last night. I would have called you myself, but I fell asleep waiting for you. I just woke up. I was worried."

"Jake, I did call you. A woman answered your phone. She said you were in the shower." There is accusation and hurt in my tone.

There's silence on the phone and I think I hear him swear, but it sounds as if he's covered the mouthpiece with his hand. "Christ. Evie. I'm sorry. I had a couple friends from the office back here for after dinner drinks, and I think my co-worker's wife must have answered my phone. I got in the shower because I had an early meeting this morning and I was trying to give them the hint to leave. Why she would answer my cell, I'm not sure. I'll talk to her. Are you upset?"

I'm silent for a second. "If that's the truth, Jake, then no, I'm not upset. I just don't see why she would pick up your cell phone and then not leave you the message."

"I don't know either, but they were drinking so that's my only guess. I'm sorry, baby. You must have been hurt."

I don't answer him for a second, but then I say, "I was confused, Jake. It's okay. If that's what happened then it's not your fault."

He lets out a shaky breath. "I miss you. I can't wait to see you. Am I still picking you up after work tonight?" He sounds worried.

"Yes," I say. "I'll see you then, okay?"

"Okay. Evie, I've . . . I've really missed you. I know it's just been a couple days, but I, I'm just really looking forward to seeing you."

I melt just a little. "Me too, Jake. See you tonight."

I hang up and roll over. I'm not sure what to feel. I wish I were more experienced at this. I take a deep breath. I either have to decide to trust him or not. I sit up, swing my legs over the bed, and stand up. Might as well start the day. I'm sure as hell not falling back to sleep now.

****

When I walk out of work later that night, Jake is waiting for me, leaning against his car, wearing a dark gray suit and a pair of aviator sunglasses. He grins when he sees me, flashing those perfect, white teeth. *Good God he's sexy.*

"Hi," I say, smiling as I approach him, still feeling a little bit leery after last night.

"Hi," he says back, still grinning.

We stand there smiling at each other goofily for a couple seconds and then we both burst out laughing and he swoops me up in his arms saying, "God, I missed you. I missed your smile and," he sticks his nose in my neck and inhales, "your smell, your body against mine at night."

"I missed you, too," I say quietly.

"You hungry?" he asks.

"Yeah, starving."

"Do you like sushi? There's this great place a couple blocks from my place." He looks at me almost nervously. Jake is such a dichotomy . . . bossy and possessive one minute, and then almost unsure the next. I'm not certain what to make of it. I know I have feelings for him, but I also know that I want to know more about him.

"I do like sushi, but I can't go out dressed in my uniform."

"How about if we pick it up to-go and bring it home?"

"Sounds great."

He lets me into his car and then walks around and slides into the driver's seat. We drive to a little hole-in-the-wall restaurant and he pulls up in front. "I know it looks questionable, but it really does have the best sushi in town."

"I trust you," I say, smiling.

"What do you like?" he asks.

"Surprise me. There's not really anything I won't eat. I can even do the raw stuff."

"Brave." He winks. "Okay, I'll be back in a few."

He locks the car behind him and as he walks into the restaurant, I dial Nicole.

"Evie," she sings into the phone. God, she should really bottle that cheer of hers.

"Hey, how's it going?"

"Oh good, you know, doing laundry, mopping the floor. The glamorous life I lead is ridiculous. What's going on with you?"

I laugh. "Jake just ran in to order takeout for dinner. I'm waiting in the car. Listen, I probably don't have long, but I wanted to ask you about something."

"Of course. Shoot!"

"Well, Jake went to San Diego on business Tuesday through Wednesday. We had plans for me to call him Tuesday night and when I did, a woman answered and said he was in the shower." I hear her draw in a sharp breath.

"I know, right?" I say. "He called me at six this morning and explained it, but I just, I don't know, I wanted to run it by you to make sure I'm not being a fool here."

"How'd he explain it?" she asks quietly.

I tell her what he told me this morning.

"Hmm . . . well, that doesn't sound totally far-fetched. I guess you just have to ask yourself what your gut feeling is."

I pause for a moment, considering. "My gut feeling is that he's a really good guy and that he's into me and cares about me. I guess I also kind of feel like he was lying about the woman."

Nicole's silent for a minute and then says, "I don't know if those two things can both be true, Evie."

I sigh. "I know. I'm confused. My heart is telling me to trust him, but—"

"I don't think you can ever go wrong listening to your heart, honey. I always like to think that even if you're wrong in the end, you're *not* wrong in the end. Does that make sense?"

"Yeah." I smile a small smile and let out a breath. "Wise woman that you are."

"With that being said, I don't ever want to see you hurt. Go with your gut, but if something happens that you question, take some space to do that. Don't let him muddle your brain up with his pheromones."

I laugh. Good advice because Jake has really amazing pheromones. Then I see him coming toward the glass door exiting the restaurant. "Oh, hey, he's on his way back. Thank you, Nic. I love you."

"Love you, babe," she whispers back.

Jake slides into the car, handing a brown paper bag to me that smells delicious, and he pulls onto the road. It only takes five minutes before we're pulling into his garage.

We walk up to his condo hand in hand and as we enter, I immediately spot a white MacBook open on his dining table, a red bow on top. I look at him, and he's smiling an uncertain smile as he looks between the computer and me.

"Jake, you didn't—"

"Evie," he says, putting his hand up in a 'keep quiet' gesture, "don't say anything until you hear me out. I know your first thought is going to be to say no to accepting this gift, but please, just listen."

I put my hands on my hips and raise one eyebrow.

"I want to do this, but not because it's just for you, but because I think you're amazing and I think that making *your* dreams come true will spread far and wide and not only affect you, but would affect me, too, and many, many people beyond that. Please let me do this for you, Evie, and all those people out there who will be changed when they read the beautiful words that are in your soul."

My eyes tear up and I take a deep, shaky breath. "No pressure, right?" I say to Jake, laughing a little, though. I walk over to the computer and start examining it, lifting the top, turning it on and watching the screen light up. Then I look at Jake and say, "You make it really, really hard to say no to you. Do you know that, Jake Madsen?"

He grins at me and I stare at him for a few seconds before saying simply, "Thank you."

****

Later, after we've eaten and Jake's made love to me slowly and sweetly in front of the fire in his living room, I get up and turn on my computer to check it out further. I grin over at Jake who has moved to the couch and is watching the news on television. He smiles back and asks, "Checking it out? Ever used a Mac?"

"No, but I've always been pretty good with computers. I'll probably get the hang of it pretty quickly."

I explore it for ten or fifteen minutes as Jake continues to watch the news show that's on. Eventually, I turn on the Internet and go to my email, which I rarely ever check. As expected, there's nothing there except some spam. I look over at Jake quickly. He's immersed in the show and so I go to Google and type in his name.

I note quickly that many of the stories are about Jake taking over his company. I don't focus on those, though. I focus on the story at the top, which is about a dinner benefit that was held in San Diego on Tuesday evening, the night the woman answered his phone. There are pictures of Jake there, talking to several older men, looking casual and gorgeous. I scroll to the last picture in the article and I freeze. It's Jake and Gwen, looking more beautiful than any couple has the right to, looking like they were made to be together. Gwen is laughing, and Jake is leaned toward her, smiling and obviously saying something funny and intimate.

I snap my computer closed, and Jake looks over. When he notes the expression on my face, he stands up. "What's wrong, baby?" he asks.

I walk over to the door and start pulling my coat on.

"Evie!" he says, sounding confused and frantic. "What happened? Why are you leaving?"

"That woman in your hotel room was Gwen, wasn't it, Jake?"

"What?" he furrows his brow. "No. Of course it wasn't. Do you think I would invite Gwen to my hotel room for drinks after the way she treated you?"

"Well, I wasn't exactly thinking you brought her to your hotel room for *drinks*, Jake. All I know is that you sure did look cozy whispering in her ear in the pictures from the benefit you were at Tuesday night."

He looks confused for a minute and then he runs his hand through his hair saying, "Evie, that was a company benefit. Gwen was there with her father. She tried to talk to me several times and I wouldn't have much to do with her. When she cornered me in front of a photographer, I leaned in and told her she was lucky that I wasn't the type to want to air my dislike for someone on film. She laughed as if I was joking, which I wasn't. That was that. I didn't talk to her again all evening."

I stare at him, my jacket half on and half off, hurt, confusion, and uncertainty warring within me. I take a deep breath. "I want to believe you, Jake, I just . . . I don't want to—"

"Evie, listen, God, if you only knew . . ." He trails off, laughing a humorless laugh.

"If I only knew what?"

His eyes meet mine and I'm stunned by the desperation I see in his expression. But is it real? "If you only knew how ridiculous it is for you to think that I would ever betray you, much less with Gwen. Really, if you could get inside my brain, you'd be laughing, too."

"Jake—"

"Please, just trust me, please don't go." His eyes are filled with something that looks like longing.

I look at him closely to judge his sincerity and I sense he's telling the truth. So I let him lead me away from his foyer area, taking off my coat, and throwing it back on the bench near his door. I follow Jake and my heart once again. But hoping deep inside, that that doesn't make me a fool.

CHAPTER TWENTY

I work another catering job on Thursday, returning home late. I'm exhausted as I crawl into bed, but the money is good, and I appreciate the feeling of safety being ahead financially brings.

On Friday, Jake asks me to stay with him and when I walk into his condo at seven thirty, having been dropped off by a co-worker since Jake had an errand to run, he scoops me up and kisses me, saying, "I'm running a bath for you so you can get a second wind because I'm taking you out dancing tonight."

"Dancing?" I sputter. "I don't know how to dance."

"Yes you do. You just don't know it. Have you ever been to a nightclub?"

"No, I've been to bars, but—"

"It's not right that a twenty-two-year-old girl has never been out dancing. I want to be the first to take you. I want to have as many firsts with you as possible." He grins at me.

"You do realize that I have to work tomorrow, right?"

"I won't have you out too late."

"Hmm . . . Okay, well then there's only one flaw in your plan. I have nothing to wear to a nightclub."

He grins a sneaky grin. "Go look on the bed."

"Jake," I put my hands on my hips, "you don't need to buy me clothes."

"Indulge me, Evie. I bought you one dress and some shoes. It means something to me to do that. Please accept it."

I raise an eyebrow at him but head toward the bedroom to check it out anyway. What in the world would Jake pick out for me to wear to a nightclub?

I walk in his room and lying on the bed is a one-shoulder, sexy, little peacock-blue number, with an edgy black-belted waist, and a pair of stiletto black heels that Nicole would drool over. I finger the silky material and I have to admit, I love it all.

I turn around and Jake's leaning casually in the doorway, one hip resting on the frame, arms crossed, and a small, satisfied smile on his face.

I smile. "I love it. Thank you. Did you really pick this out?"

He grins. "Well, I had some help from a saleswoman at Saks. But I did give her the color scheme I wanted, and I looked at the clothes you left here for your size."

"Peacock-blue, huh?" I raise an eyebrow.

He shrugs. "I like the color. Just don't ask me to take you anywhere near the zoo."

I laugh and then kiss him quickly, before I head to the bathroom to peel off my dirty work clothes. Jake runs me a bath and then heads to the kitchen to throw together a quick dinner for me since he's already eaten.

I soak in the lavender-scented bubble bath Jake bought for me, turning on the jets to high. After about twenty minutes, my body and my mind feel rejuvenated, and I pull myself out of the cooling water and start getting ready.

I pull on a black thong and then dress in the outfit Jake bought for me. The dress fits perfectly, although it's very sexy, clinging to every curve I have. I'm not that big on top, but I have a small waist and long legs and even I can see that this dress flatters me.

I blow dry my hair and curl it in loose waves. I up the drama of my usual makeup with a darker, smokier eye and some nude lip gloss.

When I walk out to the kitchen, Jake turns around and his body stills as his eyes roam over me, filling with heat. "You're stunning."

I smile, fidgeting a little. "Thank you. I have a personal shopper who's well acquainted with my figure."

He grins at me and places a bowl on the counter. "Pasta Primavera with shrimp," he says.

I sit down and dig in saying through the first mouthful, "Oh God, this is delicious. Did you make this from scratch?"

"There's nothing to that dish. Chopping some vegetables and boiling some pasta."

I don't buy it. It's way too delicious. "I'm going to cook for you next. You've spoiled me enough already."

"Get used to it. I like spoiling you."

Then he takes off the long-sleeved, cotton pullover he's wearing and I freeze. The white T-shirt he's wearing underneath has a big stamp across the front that says, *World's Greatest* in bold, black print.

I almost choke on my food, snorting, and quickly bring my napkin up to my mouth so I don't spew pasta all over him.

"What?" he says innocently.

I point at his shirt. "World's Greatest *what?*" I ask, trying to rein in my laughter.

"Oh, this?" he asks, pointing to his chest. "It's all inclusive. *World's Greatest Guy, World's Greatest Lover, World's Greatest Cook.*" He motions to my pasta when he says this last part. "You name it, I'm the greatest."

I grin. "Ah. Well, I do appreciate your confidence. But you know, you've left yourself wide open now for your critics to test you."

He leans on the counter, smiling devilishly at me. "I only care about one critic. And I'm looking forward to being tested. The more testing, the better. Lots of testing would be good." He winks.

I grin again. "You're completely ridiculous, you do realize that, right?"

He laughs out loud. "Finish up. I'm going to go change while you're eating and then we'll get going."

"You're not going to wear your *World's Greatest* shirt to the club?" I yell down the hall.

"You don't really want me to advertise all over town, do you?" he calls back and I can hear the smile in his voice.

He emerges ten minutes later in a pair of black slacks and a pale gray, button down shirt, a black belt and shoes. *Yum.*

****

The downtown nightclub that Jake takes me to is stylish and trendy, with a New York City loft vibe.

We get lucky and snag a table near the bar just as a small group is leaving. Jake pulls out my chair for me and when the cocktail waitress comes over, he orders a water for himself and I order a glass of chardonnay. The waitress doesn't even look at me. She's so busy staring at Jake, I wonder if she even heard my order. But five minutes later she's back with my wine and I can only shake my head.

Jake pulls his chair around so he's right next to me and he nuzzles into my neck, flirting, and making me laugh as we chat and I sip my wine.

I look around at the beautiful, modern decor and think about how Landon would think this place is hot. He's always talking about the clubs he's gone to on trips to New York and L.A. I wonder out loud if he's been here.

"Why don't you text him and see if he wants to join us?"

I look at Jake, surprised. "Really?"

"Yeah, I'd love to hang out with your friends."

I hesitate, but why not? "Okay," I say pulling out my phone and shooting Landon a quick text.

He texts me back a few minutes later and says he's just finishing up dinner with a friend, but that they'd love to meet us.

Forty-five minutes later, I see Landon walk in and I stand up, waving excitedly at him. He rushes over, a dark-haired guy trailing right behind him. When he's almost to our table, he yells, "Fancy Face!" and I rush into his arms yelling, "Hi!" over the hubbub of the club.

He lets me go, saying loudly, "Girl, you look hot." Then he looks over to Jake who is standing and shakes his hand, saying, "Thanks for inviting us." Jake smiles and nods at him, saying, "It's good to officially meet you."

He pulls the good-looking guy behind him to his side and introduces him as Jeff Stoltz. I take him in, thinking he looks really familiar, and when it hits me, the hair color is different but . . . "Has anyone ever told you you look—"

"Like Matt Damon?" he finishes, smiling. "Yeah, I've heard that once or twice."

"That often, huh?" I laugh and gesture for them to sit, which they do.

As Jeff is ordering drinks, and Jake looks away, Landon catches my eye and fans himself, shooting looks in Jake's direction. I grin. But I can't disagree.

We order more drinks and chat easily. Jake is charming and personable and I'm having a great time.

I have three glasses of wine in me when Jake stands up, pulling me with him and whispering, "I want you on the dance floor."

My heart starts beating a little bit faster and I sway slightly, but suddenly, dancing doesn't seem quite so daunting. I have a sneaking suspicion that the three glasses of wine I've consumed is the reason for this.

I wave to the guys and follow Jake onto the dance floor. A mix of Maroon Five's "One More Night" is blasting through the speakers, and suddenly, I'm in Jake's arms and he's moving against me, and it's easy to follow his sexy hip movements. I bring my arms up around his neck and we move against each other, and besides having sex with Jake, this is the most erotic thing I've ever experienced.

"I should have known you'd be a good dancer," I whisper into his ear.

He smiles and presses more fully into my body, making me close my eyes and cling more tightly to his neck. Would it be considered déclassé to have an orgasm on the dance floor of a nightclub? I giggle to myself. Okay, maybe I've had just a tad *too much* to drink.

The song changes, and I feel a tap on my shoulder and Landon is grinning at me. Jake takes my jaw in his hand and kisses me hard and quick on the mouth, turning me over to Lan. "I'm gonna go use the restroom," he says. "Take care of her." Landon nods and then spins me around as I giggle and follow his lead.

"Jeff seems nice, Lan," I say, spinning back into him.

"He is. I might really like him. I wanted you to hang out with him a little bit so you could give me your impression," he says, looking a little nervous.

"I like him a lot so far."

"Good. I think he's great. And hot. I mean, maybe not as hot as your boy toy, but hot." He laughs, spinning me again.

"Where'd you meet him?"

"At Starbucks. It was crowded and he asked if he could share my table. We ended up talking for three hours."

"I love that." I grin at him, spinning away. I kinda love everything tonight. The buzz of the wine, the beat of the music, having one of my best friends to laugh with, being here with Jake, being in his arms . . .

Ten minutes later, just as I'm starting to believe I might be a truly gifted dancer, or maybe it's just the wine, I'm not really sure, a big dark-haired guy in a tight black T-shirt grabs my hand and tries to pull me into him. I shake my head no, pointing at Landon, and when Landon sees what's going on, he grabs my hand and attempts to pull me back. Apparently, this guy isn't going to take two "no"s for an answer, though, because he tugs me harder, and I go stumbling against his body. There's a slight struggle as Landon tries to pull me away from him, and the beefy guy in black tries to turn my body so he can put his massive frame between Landon and me. I look up into his face and can see he's had way too much to drink.

Suddenly, the guy who has hold of me is flying backward, and I catch sight of a livid-looking Jake, his hand on the back of the guy's collar, hauling him to the edge of the floor. Jake says something close to his face, and the guy raises his hands in a mock surrender and goes stumbling away. I stand still, looking at Jake's angry face. *That expression* . . .

Jake watches him leave, his jaw tense, and then returns to me. I feel slightly off balance. It must be the alcohol. I shake it off and smile brightly at Jake. "My hero," I croon and when Jake looks down into my face, he must see I'm really tipsy because he shakes his head slightly, smiles, and puts his arms back around me. I grin up at him and we start moving again.

An hour later, I'm sweaty and breathing hard, and my feet are killing me.

Jeff joined us on the floor a few minutes after Jake hauled the big guy off me, and we've all been having a blast together.

Jake leans forward and says something to Landon and Landon nods, blowing a kiss my way, which I return. I wave at Jeff and he waves back. Then Jake takes my hand and leads me off the dance floor.

I ask him to wait for a second as I use the restroom and then give him a quick kiss as I head inside. After I do my business and freshen up at the mirror, I walk out. I look around, confused. Jake is nowhere in sight. I finally spot him by the door, his face tight as he talks closely to a woman I can't see completely because her head is turned, and there's someone standing behind her obscuring most of her body. All I can make out is brownish hair that's pulled up and long, shapely legs. She turns and walks out the door, and he looks toward the restrooms, a nervous expression on his face. He doesn't see me because I'm already coming toward him, squeezing through a group of people by the bar.

He goes over to the bouncer and says something to him quickly and then as he looks up and sees me approaching him, his face registers a fleeting look of surprise, but then softens and he takes my hand.

"Ready?" he says.

"Who were you talking to?" I ask, frowning slightly.

He looks at me and pauses for a second before answering. "Just some woman who was drunk, making a scene. The bouncers called her a cab and I just lead her to the door. Hold on, let me get a glass of water for you at the bar before we leave."

"I'm okay," I say. "You looked mad."

"Not really. She was just being kind of belligerent. She tried to make a pass. I said no. That was that." He tugs gently on my hand.

"Now trust me on the water. You'll be glad you drank it tomorrow morning, especially since you're working." He orders a water when we get to the bar and then watches as I suck the whole thing down. I smile up at him when I'm done, putting the glass on the bar.

"Take me home," I say smiling. "Before I have to beat more women off you." He laughs, shaking his head.

We walk to the door and Jake leans in and says something to the bouncer, and within minutes, the bouncer signals to Jake and the valet is bringing his car around, and we're on our way home. He seems a little tense for a few minutes, but as we laugh about Landon's hilariously dramatic dance moves, he relaxes. We reminisce about how he was doing them to crack us up, lip-synching, and being completely over the top. I don't think I've laughed that much, *ever*.

When we pull into Jake's garage, he shuts off his car, and instead of getting out, he looks over at me and takes my face in his hands and starts kissing me, deep and wet. He feels so good, and I'm kissing him back with equal enthusiasm when he pulls me on top of him, and I press down and that feels *great* and so I keep doing it. Suddenly, I hear the sound of material tearing. We both stop, confused, and when I pull slightly off Jake, I realize that the seam at his crotch is torn straight down the middle, gaping open. "Oh my God," I breathe. "Your boy part is like the Incredible Hulk."

He raises an eyebrow. "Boy part?"

I nod slowly. "Is he angry?"

"Not yet. But if you keep referring to him as a 'boy part,' he could get there. He's all man. You don't want to see him get angry."

"Oh, I definitely want to see him get angry."

He laughs out loud and then says, "Come on, let's get you upstairs."

He helps me out of the car and then leads me toward the entrance to the lobby. As we walk past the front desk, Jake places me directly in front of him to hide his torn pants and walks pressed against me, saying, "Hey Joe," as the night deskman looks at us, a confused expression on his face. I get a fit of the giggles and Jake rushes me to the elevator, practically pushing me inside and then following quickly. I laugh all the way upstairs.

When we get inside Jake's apartment, we stumble against his wall, still laughing. Jake's body presses against me. As I watch his beautiful face smiling at me, I turn serious. "Jake, I've never really been silly a lot in my life and so I want to thank you for that. I know that sounds kind of crazy and maybe even a little dumb, but, really, it's a big deal to me so, honestly, thank you for tonight." I blink at him, suddenly feeling just a little bit emotional. There's no way he could know, but after only such a short time, he's given me so much that I've always, always wanted, but never had.

He's looking at me seriously now, too, as if he completely understands. "I look forward to lots more silly moments with you, beautiful." His eyes roam over my face, filled with warmth and satisfaction.

Then his mouth comes down on mine as he presses me harder against the wall. We kiss for long moments, Jake's tongue plundering my mouth as I moan and whimper, the taste of him dizzying, even though I'm mostly sober now.

He lifts me off my feet and I wrap my legs around him. I reach down and put my hand into his already torn pants, stroking him as best as I can with our bodies pressed so closely together. He lets out a low growl, and I feel moisture trickle between my legs at the sound of it.

He takes one of his hands off my ass, pressing me harder against the wall as he reaches down and tears my thong right off me. My eyes snap open as I take in a sharp breath at the surprise of it, and then moan as he fingers my opening.

"Always so wet for me," he chokes out. I lean my head back against the wall as he licks and kisses up my throat and it feels so amazing that I'm writhing against him, moving my core against the huge erection I can feel pressed tightly against me.

When Jake leans his hips back, I whimper in protest.

"Take my cock out, Evie," he growls, and I reach down, through the tear in his pants, into his boxers, doing as he says, springing him free.

He grips my ass tighter as he slams foreword, impaling me against the wall, and I cry out as he fills and stretches me, my internal muscles tightening around his shaft. For several seconds, we just stare into each other's eyes, and the heat and intensity coming from his has me mesmerized.

He keeps looking straight at me as he slowly pulls back, almost withdrawing completely and then slamming back into me, pressing against the part of me that needs it most. *Oh God that feels so good*. My eyes close involuntarily and I moan deeply, my lips parting. I hear Jake let out a guttural hiss.

That's when things get intense.

Jake crashes his mouth down on mine and begins thrusting into me, hard and deep, almost punishing, my back slams against the wall. But I love every minute of it, feeling owned by this beautiful man, hammering into me, too far gone to be gentle.

He reaches down between us and presses his finger against my clit, and I start panting and moaning into his mouth as an orgasm crashes and rolls through me.

He rips his mouth from mine as he growls, "Mine. Only mine. Only. Ever. Mine," still slamming into me, pounding me against the wall. He looks primal, out of control. His eyes close and his lips part as his orgasm builds, and then he throws his head back, letting out a deep moan as I feel his hot seed jetting inside me.

He looks back at me lazily as he glides in and out slowly, drawing out the pleasure of his climax.

I blurt out, "You are so beautiful."

He smiles at me, his eyes warm as he lets me down to the floor. His arms must be killing him.

"You're the beautiful one."

I kiss him sweetly on the lips, and then we adjust our clothing, and he takes my hand and leads me to bed.

CHAPTER TWENTY-ONE

On Saturday morning, surprisingly, I wake up feeling pretty good, which I'm thankful for since my shift starts at ten o'clock. I take a shower, which I needed badly as Jake and I had pretty much fallen into bed last night after the dancing and the wall activities. I smile at the memory. I blow my hair partially dry, and put it in a loose braid that falls over my shoulder, apply light makeup, and pull on my uniform. I kiss Jake goodbye and nuzzle into his neck as I lean over him. He growls and says, "Don't tempt me. I'm three seconds away from making you very late for work." I giggle, and give him one more quick kiss on the cheek, leaving him in bed. I look back at him once before I walk out the door, lying on his back, tangled in the sheets. No one should look that gorgeous first thing in the morning. It's just not right. I smile to myself.

Jake arranged one of his company cars to pick me up at his building, and it's waiting for me at the curb as I step outside. I don't mind the bus, but I could get used to this. It takes less than ten minutes before I'm clocking in.

The day goes by quickly even though I'm tired from our late night and lots of physical exertion. Before we fell into bed last night, Jake and I had made plans for him to pick me up from work. But close to the end of my shift, my manager asks if I want to leave an hour early because of an over-scheduling issue, and I jump at it.

I text Jake, but he doesn't text me back by the time I'm clocking out, and so I change my clothes quickly, and then ask one of the other girls leaving at the same time if she'd mind dropping me at his place.

She drops me in front of his building, and I try calling him one more time, but he doesn't answer. I call to someone entering to hold the door and go in behind him. I get on the penthouse elevator alone, and since I remember the simple code Jake used to get to his floor, I punch that in. I hope he doesn't mind me coming over early, but why would he? What if he's not home? Darn, I guess I'll come downstairs and wait in the lobby and just keep calling him. There's probably a coffee shop somewhere close by.

The elevator opens and I notice that the door to his condo is open a little bit, and I hear voices coming from inside. I frown a little and stop to the side of the door, unsure now if I should knock. I decide to anyway, but as I lift my hand, I hear a woman say, "You don't have to act like this. Let me make it better, honey." I freeze. *What the hell?*

Jake responds and his voice sounds clipped, angry, "Don't start this shit. I explained to you in San Diego the nature of our relationship and that is that there isn't one, okay?"

"You lie to yourself, Jake. You can't just make this go away. You can't just make *me* go away."

"The fuck I can't. Get out."

There's silence for a couple seconds, and then I hear a rustling and Jake yells, "Get the fuck OUT!" and it sounds like the woman is sniffling.

Footsteps come toward the door and I panic. *Shit!* What should I do? Before I can even come up with any sort of plan, the door is flung open and I'm staring into Jake's seriously livid eyes. He sees me and a look of shock runs over his features before he says under his breath, "Shit. Evie. What the *fuck* are you doing here?"

It feels like a rock drops into my stomach. I stand there gaping at him like a stupid fish, when a woman walks out his door. She's gorgeous, with thick, light brown hair to her shoulders and big, green eyes. She's older than Jake and me, probably in her late thirties. She looks at me, and then looks at Jake, and then looks back at me with a look of scorn on her face.

"Really, Jake? Already?" she clips out.

Jake closes his eyes for a second and then repeats in a barely controlled voice, "Get out."

She ignores him and walks over to me and extends her hand. "I'm Lauren," she says, but the way she says it, I can tell she's anything but happy to meet me.

I have no idea what to do, and so I take her hand, whispering, "Nice to meet you, I'm—"

"Mom!" Jake yells. "If you don't get out, swear to God, I will call security to haul you downstairs." Jake is clenching his jaw and his hands are fisted at his sides.

Mom?

I'm flabbergasted, and my mouth opens and closes stupidly again. I guess I really underestimated her age because she seriously doesn't look a day over thirty-five. I guess that's what money can do for you.

A look of hurt passes over Lauren's face, but she pulls herself taller and says, "Fine, Jake, have it your way." Then as she's stepping on to the elevator, she turns and looks at me and says, "You're just one of many. You should know that."

Hurt slams into me and I gasp as the elevator door closes and I lean to my right so that the wall will hold me up.

What the . . . ?

Jake is standing just outside his doorway, staring straight ahead, unmoving except the continued clenching of his jaw.

I walk over to the elevator and push the down button, and that seems to snap him out of it because he takes three big steps over to me and puts his hand on my arm and says, "Evie! Where are you going?" He looks desperate now.

"I'm leaving, Jake. Obviously you don't want me here. I'm sorry, I got off work early and I thought, I mean, I thought it would be okay. I called you . . ." I trail off, my eyes filling with tears because I feel stupid and confused.

"Evie, baby, please. Let me explain. I'm so sorry. So fucking sorry.

I keep messing up." He runs his hand through his hair and looks like such an uncertain little boy. I crumble, *again*. I let him guide me into his condo so he can tell me what the *hell* that was. I leave my jacket and my bag by the door, though, in case I need to leave quickly.

****

Jake closes his door and leads me to his living room area. He pulls up a leather-upholstered ottoman, moves it in front of the couch, then pulls me down to sit knee to knee with him. He takes both my hands in his. "First of all, I'm so sorry I made you feel badly for coming here. You can show up here anytime you want to. I never expected my mom to . . ." He sighs. "We're . . . estranged. Things are not good between us, which I guess you could tell." He lets out something that sounds like a strangled laugh. "I had no idea she was coming here today. The last time I saw her I told her I didn't want anything to do with her, and I meant *ever*."

I blink at him, not saying anything, waiting for him to continue. "It's complicated, but, my mom has issues, serious issues, and she made my home life a living hell. She's the reason that I acted out the way I did when I was a teenager, and she's the reason for the stilted relationship between my dad and me."

He looks into my eyes, his filled with sadness. "When I saw you standing there, I couldn't believe that you were even about to share her *air*. She's a ruthless bitch, and she'll do or say anything that she thinks will further her own agenda. I wasn't mad that you were here, I was mad that you were even in the *vicinity* of that pit viper. And that was not your fault, but I lost it, and I'm so sorry." His eyes are pleading.

I look down at our joined hands and then back up at him as he continues, "She only made that comment to you about being one of many because she was being vindictive since I was throwing her out. She doesn't even know you, Evie. And she sure as shit doesn't know anything important about me."

"Jake," I say, squeezing his hands. "I feel like when you're talking about yourself, you're talking to me in code. I get the gist of what you're saying, but you really haven't told me anything."

He sighs. "I'll give you some examples. Just give me some time, okay? This is stuff I've never talked about to anyone and it's hard for me to get into. I've spent so many years trying to pretend it doesn't exist. I know that's not the healthy thing to do. But just . . . trust me, okay? Can you do that?" He's looking at me desperately, like my answer means his life or death. Can I? Should I? Do I trust this man?

I say the first thing that pops into my head. "Okay, Jake. I trust you." And despite all my doubts, I do, I honestly do, and that makes me happy as much as it scares the hell out of me. Nothing makes sense anymore.

He's holding back. Questionable things keep coming up. I shouldn't feel safe with him. And yet, I do. I have to wonder about my own judgment.

"Can you just tell me one thing, though? Why is she in town?"

"Part of it is because my father changed his will in the hospital and left me the company and she's not happy about that. She's here, in part, to make an appeal to the board. It won't work, but she'll give it her best. Mostly, it's a way to control me and she's angry that she's lost that."

I nod slowly, creasing my brow. We're both silent for several seconds before he continues. "Forgive me for talking to you like that, for making you feel that way? God, for that whole fucked-up situation?" He looks at me sadly.

I take a deep breath. "Yes, I forgive you. And you don't have to apologize for your mom, Jake. I know better than anyone you can't help who your parents are."

He looks into my eyes and nods. "Thank you," he says, looking down at our hands and then bringing them up and kissing my knuckles one at a time. "I never want to do anything to hurt you, Evie. Everything I do, it's because my feelings are so strong for you . . . I . . . Christ, I'm so out of my element here, and there are all these fucked up things . . . Just, be patient with me?"

I wonder for a minute if he's going to tear up, but he just looks at me sadly and finally, I do the only thing that feels right. I put my arms around him and hold him close. I feel his body relax into mine.

CHAPTER TWENTY-TWO

Jake grabs a menu from a Chinese restaurant down the street, and I look it over and then tell him what I want - chicken with broccoli and an egg roll.

He calls in the order and I ask him if he'd mind if I took a quick shower before dinner. Cleaning hotel rooms all day doesn't exactly make me feel fresh and clean.

"Of course," he says. "You don't have to ask. My home is your home, okay?" He looks at me like it's really important to him that I understand that.

"Okay, Jake."

I take a quick shower and change into a tank top and a pair of shorts. I brush out my hair and leave it down.

I walk back out into the kitchen/living area and don't see Jake. The door leading to the balcony is open, though, and so I go there and peek out. Jake is standing against the low wall with his hands on the ledge looking out to the city.

I walk up behind him and wrap my arms around his waist, laying my head against his back. He takes my hands in his from the front and inhales a deep breath. As much as I'm rattled by my run in with his mom, I feel like he needs me more than I need him right now. I'm not new to feeling empathy for people for the parental hand they were dealt. I grew up in the foster care system. But I never expected that Jake's situation was so extreme he had to kick his own mom out of his life, literally and figuratively.

After a couple minutes, I give him a gentle squeeze and then slide my hands up the bottom of his shirt, leaning down and kissing the base of his back, and licking up his spine a little ways. I smile against his skin.

As I start lifting the back of his shirt a little more, his body tenses and I pause, wondering if I'm doing something wrong. I realize quickly that I've never actually seen his back and I wonder briefly if maybe he has scars there, too . . . but I don't remember feeling anything when we were in bed . . .

Then the moment passes as he draws in air and turns around so that my face is now at his stomach, which I press my lips against. "Evie," he breathes.

He leans back against the half wall, and I go down on my knees in front of him, unbuttoning the top of his jeans. I smile up at him and his eyes are dark and filled with need.

Jake's lips are parted and at the look of blatant lust on his face, I feel wetness between my legs. I press my thighs together, relishing the sensation.

Along with the butterflies that take flight in my stomach are wisps of excitement, thrilling and heady. *Am I really about to do this?*

I unzip his jeans and drag them down his legs, moving slowly as I mentally prepare for this. Next, I pull his boxers down and his beautiful cock springs free, rock hard. I look up at him and his arms are spread, braced on the wall as he leans back, resting his ass against the stone. I must look a little unsure because he says, "Put your mouth on me, please, Evie." His need makes me bolder, as if there's no way I can do this wrong.

He's perfection, his body taut with desire, heavy with arousal, and my mouth waters at the sight of him.

I don't know if I'm going to be any good at this, but I decide to go for gusto. I'm so turned on that when I lick up the underside of his erection, I'm the one to moan. I breathe in his scent, clean and woodsy, but also something muskier down here. It's all Jake and I love it.

My lips stretch over the wide crown, sucking gently. I flutter my tongue across the underside, loving the feel of his soft skin. Jake rewards me with a loud moan, rolling his hips gently.

I fist the base of him with one hand and draw him deeper into my mouth and start sucking rhythmically.

"Oh, fuck," he groans. "Evie . . . your mouth . . . like that," Jake grinds out. He pushes his hands into my hair, pulling at the roots. It should hurt, but strangely, I love the feel of it and it spurs me on.

I keep sucking and stroking him with my mouth while my hand jacks him from below, like he showed me.

I feel him swell in my mouth and I let out another moan, as he starts thrusting his hips, fucking my mouth, directing my movement. I love that he's lost control. I love that I've done that to him.

"Oh God, I'm gonna come, baby." I keep sucking him, though, working my lips and tongue hungrily, desperate to bring him to orgasm.

I feel the first spurts of semen in my mouth, thick and salty, and I swallow all of it, milking him with my mouth until his last shudder.

"Holy fuck." His voice is still hoarse with passion.

I tuck him back into his pants just as the buzzer from the front desk sounds. It's our food.

We both look at the door at the same time and burst out laughing, him running his hand through his hair and muttering, "Holy shit. Seriously, unleashed a sex demon."

I giggle and he pulls me up, kissing me quickly on the lips, and I follow him back into the condo.

****

We eat our takeout on the floor in the living room. Jake has a game on TV, but he's not paying much attention. We laugh and share bites and he's sweet and flirty. My Jake again. The shadow of his mother's visit seems to have faded. I guess a blowjob can distract a man from some of life's most disturbing events. *Noted.*

After dinner, Jake tells me he's going to take a quick shower. I bring the dishes into the kitchen and load the dishwasher. As I'm straightening his pile of mail, Jake comes up behind me and turns me around, lifting me easily onto the counter. His hand grips the back of my neck and my legs open for him, allowing him to press his body fully into me. He smiles and then kisses me slowly and deeply as my hands run up and down the hard muscles of his back.

"Well, hello," I say, smiling, when he breaks the kiss. "How was your shower?"

"Good," he says, nipping at my lip. "I missed you, though."

"We'll have to schedule a shower for the both of us then. I look forward to getting wet with you, Jake Madsen." I smile my best saucy smile.

A strange look passes over his face, but he schools it quickly, smiling and saying, "Oh, I have a whole spreadsheet of things I plan to do with you."

"A whole spreadsheet, huh?" I say smiling back, convincing myself that I imagined the strange look.

"Mmm," he murmurs, rubbing his nose against mine. "Color-coded and everything."

"Well, by all means, then, let's start working our way through that." I grin down at him.

He kisses me again, but now it's harder, more demanding. In minutes, we're panting and gripping at each other, hands everywhere.

I feel lost. Needy. My panties already drenched with arousal, my nipples pebbled against his hard chest.

I let out a whimper as Jake pulls the strap of my tank top down one shoulder, looking at me with dark, hooded eyes. He licks his lips as he pulls the other strap down to bare my breasts, and the throbbing between my legs intensifies. "Please, Jake," I whisper, and I'm not even entirely sure what I'm asking him for.

"What do you need, baby? Tell me."

"More," I say simply, and his slow, sexy smile has more moisture trickling down to my core.

His hands cup my breasts, and he brushes his thumbs over my nipples, and I moan as they tighten even more, shooting a bolt of electricity between my legs, my sex clenching. My head falls back, my mouth opening as he takes turns at my nipples, sucking them and flicking them with his tongue expertly.

Jake's mouth pops off my nipple and he steps back. I whimper at the loss of him, taking in his tented jeans and his lust-filled eyes. He scoops me off the counter and throws me over his shoulder. I shriek, laughing as Jake strides to his bedroom. He throws me on the bed, and now I let out another little scream, still laughing as he pounces on me, grinning.

But then he leans up off me and the look on his face becomes serious. "You are so beautiful, Evelyn Cruise."

I smile up at him, thinking I'm nowhere near as beautiful as he is right now—looking down at me, the moonlight shining in on him.

My thighs open to accommodate him and I stare into his eyes. "Show me."

He kisses my mouth, slowly. It's sexy and tormenting at this point because I'm so turned on. My hips press upward and Jake reaches down my shorts, between my legs and moans, "God, Evie, you're drenched."

He stands up and I watch him strip off his T-shirt, followed by his jeans and boxers. I take in his hard, male perfection, and then he grabs my hips and pulls me to the side of the bed so that my ass is right at the edge. He pulls my shorts and panties down my legs, and then does the same with my tank top, which is still pulled down around my waist.

The bed is the perfect height for him to remain standing, and when I feel his throbbing cock at my entrance, I whimper with pleasure. He takes himself in his hand and uses his erection to rub against my clit and I think I might come right then and there. He circles his erection slowly against my sex, teasing and torturing me, bringing me close to the edge, but not giving me enough to tip me over.

"Jake," I whine, desperate with need.

He chuckles, but then positions himself and surges inside me. I gasp, my body gripping him, getting used to his size, before relaxing just as he starts moving. He groans loudly. "God, Evie. You're so tight, so hot, you feel amazing."

He starts pumping into me, and from this angle, every thrust causes his body to hit my clit.

"Harder," I breathe, tilting my ass so he can go deeper, giving greater access to his thrusts, completely lost in his possession.

He groans, thrusting harder, and I can feel pressure in my core building as he continues to pump into me over and over again. I sit up slightly and grab his contracting ass, amazed at the feeling of his muscles, hard as stone. Then he brings one hand down between my legs and presses his thumb against my clit, and that's all it takes to send me spiraling into an orgasm, my sex pulsing around his cock.

I come down slowly, Jake still pumping inside me, and then watch him dazedly as his own orgasm takes over and he rams into me, his eyes closing and his lips parting in pleasure, filling me with scalding heat. And I seriously feel aftershocks just at the expression on his face alone. *I'll never stop loving that look.*

Jake falls forward, shuddering as he plants his face into my neck. We both breathe hard for several long minutes until he pulls out of me and kisses me slowly and deeply. Then he rolls to the side so we're lying next to each other.

That was so amazing. I think I might die. For real.

When I look over at him, he's smiling up at the ceiling. "What's that for?" I ask, smiling, too.

"I knew it'd be like this with us," he says.

"You did, did you?"

"Yup. Knew it the first time I kissed you."

I smile at him and lean up to kiss his lips gently. "I'm gonna go clean up. I'll be right back."

When I finish in the bathroom, Jake is already under the covers, wearing his boxers and T-shirt. I snuggle in against him, and we whisper and cuddle until both of us fall asleep.

CHAPTER TWENTY-THREE

Evie is Fourteen, Leo is Fifteen

I smile up at the sky as Leo makes his way to me on what I've come to think of as "our roof." I keep staring upward as I say teasingly, "Hark, who goes there? Is it my lion or is it my boy?"

"If I'm half of each then I can't be one or the other, I can only be both," he says with a smile in his voice.

I ponder this for a minute. "True, I suppose. But just for the record, it wouldn't matter who showed up. I love both equally."

"Aren't you afraid of the lion, just a little?"

"Uh uh," I shake my head no. "In fact, the lion is my favorite—he's the side that's fierce and strong. He's the one who fights for those he loves savagely, who is powerful. He's the one who shines through when I see that fire in your eyes."

I look over at him now and there it is, that burning expression that makes my heart beat faster, in excitement and confusion both.

He stares at me for a minute, his eyes wandering down to my mouth. Then he closes his eyes and turns his head to look up at the sky.

He changes the subject. "I met with my new adoptive parents again today. Looks like I'll be moving in with them by the end of the month. Two weeks."

I turn to him, resting my head on my hand, my elbow propped on the roof. "Yeah? You still like them as much as you thought?"

"Yeah. They're . . . yeah, they seem real nice. He doesn't talk a whole lot, but he seems like a nice guy. She's kind of nervous, but nice too. She touches me a lot, trying to be motherly. I don't think they've been around teenagers a whole lot."

He's silent for a minute and then, "They also told me that it's a good possibility that he's going to take a new job in Southern California." He glances at me nervously. "It's not set in stone, but . . . they say it's likely. They went on and on about how fun it would be to live near the beach."

I feel my heart plummet to my feet. "What?" I whisper.

"Listen, it's not for sure, yet, okay? I just wanted to tell you now so that it won't come as a shock if it does happen. Listen, Evie, it might not be the worst thing in the world. I mean, one of us having a stable family . . . it will give us that much more of a chance for a successful start once you turn eighteen. We won't be so alone."

"Yeah, but that's in four YEARS, Leo! We're going to be apart for four years?"

He sighs. "I don't know. I hope not. But I'm trying to look on the bright side here, okay?"

We both stare up at the sky for long minutes before he turns to me and says, "Do you know the quality all lions possess above all else?"

"No." I shake my head.

"Loyalty," he says, smiling and showing me that adorable gap in his teeth. "No matter how far apart we are. No matter the distance or time, I will never love anyone except you. Not ever."

I nod at him sadly.

He gets a teasing glint in his eyes. "Also? They really like to maul their women." Then he play tackles me, rolling me, and growling in my ears.

I laugh and squeal, hissing, "Leo! You'll wake everyone else sleeping inside!" I roll away from him. I laugh again when he gives me a vicious look, crossing his eyes.

"You're crazy," I say, as we lie down next to each other again, holding hands. But I feel better. He's mine, and he always will be.

CHAPTER TWENTY-FOUR

The next couple of days are pretty uneventful. I stay at my own place Sunday and Monday, feeling like a little space in a new relationship is probably a good idea. Jake doesn't seem to agree, but he doesn't push.

He has to fly to the office in San Diego again for work, and he leaves on Tuesday morning so he can be in the office for meetings all day. I feel slightly anxious about him leaving because of what happened on his last trip, but I put it out of my mind as best as I can.

He calls me several times while he's traveling and between meetings, and seeing his name on my phone gives me butterflies each time. *God, I really need to get a hold of myself.* I think several times about how my relationship with Jake has traveled so far out of my safety zone. If he decides I'm not enough for him, how will I survive that? I stop and take deep breaths when these thoughts assault me, and somehow, I'm able to resist talking myself into returning to my cocoon of safety. Instead, I keep busy with work, running, and catching up on the book I was in the middle of reading and have neglected recently.

I go to lunch with Nicole on Tuesday afternoon and catch her up on my suddenly interesting life. We giggle like schoolgirls, and it feels great to share my happiness with her. I ask her questions about her relationship with Mike, things I never would have had the courage or the need to ask her about before now. Is it normal to want sex all the freaking time? Nicole: In the beginning yes; after five years of marriage and a four-year-old, not so much. Can you fall in love with someone after less than a month of knowing them? Nicole: More likely lust than love, but enjoy it all the same.

We look at our calendars and she asks if I can come over for dinner a week from Saturday. We plan it and as she hugs me outside the restaurant, she says, "Invite Jake."

"Okay," I say, smiling, looking forward to introducing him to three more of the people I love most in the world.

I call Jake at his hotel room that night and we talk for an hour before I'm so tired I can't stay awake any longer.

On Wednesday morning, I clock into work at ten and make my way up to the top floor to clean the penthouse suite. I knock three loud raps on the door and wait a minute, and when no one answers, I use my key card to let myself in. I wheel my cart in and look around confused. The place is immaculate. Clearly no one has used the room, which is weird because I know they wouldn't have me scheduled to clean it unless someone had rented it the night before.

I grab my walkie-talkie and am about to press the button to connect to my manager in his office downstairs when I hear a sound from the bedroom. I frown and call out, "Hello?" No one answers and so I take a few steps toward the room. Seriously, if there's some serial killer in there, I will totally bash him over the head with this heavy-ass walkie-talkie. Wait, those sound like really bad famous last words. I grab the spray bottle of bleach, too, just in case I need extra ammunition.

I peek around the corner, craning my neck, and what do I see? Standing in the far doorway is Jake, hands stuffed in his pockets, grinning at me.

I don't know if it's the shock of seeing him or just that I react instantly to my emotions, but I drop my "weapons," let out a happy shriek, run across the room, and launch myself at him. He catches me, laughing and spinning me around while I rain kisses over his face. I squeal, taking his face in my hands and kissing his mouth now, laughing along with him. He's kissing me back and we're acting like two people who haven't seen each other in ages. And that's how I feel. I feel like I haven't seen this man in years and years and the joy that pounds out of my chest is something I don't question. I just hold him close and relish the feeling of him being in my arms. I've missed him so much. And this is crazy. It's only been two days! But he seems to accept my reaction as perfectly normal, and he keeps kissing me, saying my name again and again, both of us caught in this strange, joyful moment. I don't look below the surface. I just soak it in.

I finally go still, but don't let go, holding him close. I close my eyes and just enjoy the throatiness of his voice against my ear, the smell of him—uniquely Jake—and the beating of his heart against my own. I can't explain it, but I know if I could freeze time right this second and live in this feeling forever, I would.

Finally, we're quiet and I slide to the ground, gazing up into his warm, brown eyes. "What are you doing here, Jake?"

"I wanted to surprise you. When we talked on Sunday, you told me you were cleaning the penthouse all this week if it was occupied and my evil wheels started turning." He grins. "I rented it on Tuesday morning before I left town. How long does it usually take to clean it?"

I furrow my brow. "You rented this room so you could spend the time with me it takes to clean it?" I say, confused.

"Yup."

Oh, okay, then.

"Um, how long to clean it? If the guests are really messy, an hour and a half?"

"They're dirty slobs."

I laugh softly. "Oh, okay, then, maybe I could push it to two hours."

He starts unzipping my dress. "What are you doing, Jake?"

"Not wasting any time."

Right.

"Um, Jake—" I start, but he's doing this thing on my neck that feels so good, I forget what I was about to say.

I take his hand and lead him to the big, upholstered chair at the other side of the room, locking the bedroom door on my way. If we got caught, it wouldn't be good. I push him down, and his eyes have already gone lazy and *God, that makes me wet.* Does he know that?

I straddle him and take his face in my hands, looking into his eyes for seconds before lowering my lips to his, nipping at him, before sliding my tongue into his mouth. Jake takes over and his kiss feels hungry and possessive. Our tongues tangle, dancing, and he brings his hands back to the zipper of my dress, yanking it down boldly. He brings it down my shoulders and I lower my arms so he can slide it down as we continue kissing. When it hits my hips, I break our kiss and stand up. Jake leans back in the chair, watching me with dark, smoldering eyes as I strip in front of him. He has one arm draped over the arm of the chair and one hand resting in his lap. His thighs are spread and his erection is tenting his black dress slacks. He looks like the epitome of every wet dream I've ever had and my core is throbbing just looking at him.

I bring the dress down over my hips and let it drop to the floor. His eyes follow the uniform and then roam back up my body. I see his cock jump in his pants, and I almost whimper with my need for him, but I manage to remain silent as I unhook my bra and let it slide down my arms and drop to the floor. My panties are next. I hook my thumbs through the waistband and drag them down my legs.

I kick off my shoes and then I stand before him, naked, letting his eyes roam over me. His look of blatant appreciation is the only thing that gives me the confidence to stand before him, on display, like I've never been before. He reaches down and unbuttons his pants and releases his zipper, letting his cock spring free. He strokes himself lazily as he continues to look at me with heated eyes, and I can't help it now, I whimper.

Oh. Dear. Heaven.

"Touch yourself, Evie," he says, his voice sounding choked, barely controlled. I'm so turned on, vibrating with need that I don't hesitate to do as he says. I bring my hands to my breasts, fingering my nipples and closing my eyes as my head falls back, mouth opening with a moan of pleasure. Then I bring one hand down to my core, slick with arousal. I rub the wetness from my opening up to my clit, moving my finger in slow circles and moaning unabashedly now.

"*Fuck*, I need to be in you now, baby," he chokes out, grabbing me by the hips and bringing me back to straddle him, my knees on the chair next to his hips. He brings me down roughly, spearing me with his hard cock, making me cry out in surprise and in pleasure as he fills me completely.

I pull up until just the tip of his cock is still in me and then I crash down on him, making him grunt and throw his head back and *God, that's so good*. I cry out, too, with the pleasure this position is giving me. Then I repeat the movement I just did, pulling up slowly and crashing down on him again.

Yes, God yes!

I picture what we must look like right now, me naked and riding him, him fully clothed beneath me, and the image in my mind makes me wild with lust.

I start moving up and down on him, mindless to anything except the race to orgasm as his mouth comes down on my breast, sucking my nipple into his mouth, almost roughly.

I throw my head back, too, and ride him enthusiastically as we both pant and groan. His hands are on my hips now, pushing me down harder and faster until we both cry out together, hot rushes of semen filling me as the waves of pleasure consume me. For a minute, I think I see stars as my orgasm peaks and then peaks again.

"Christ, fuck," Jake grunts out, taking my mouth and kissing me passionately as we both moan through our orgasms.

I kiss Jake fervently as we descend, gripping each other tightly and breathing hard.

We stay still in each other's arms for long minutes as our breathing returns to normal. I lean back and look into his face, grinning.

"What are you doing to me?" I ask, awestruck.

"What are you doing to *me*?" He grins back.

I laugh. *Uh, yeah.* I disengage myself from him and stand up, walking to the bathroom to clean myself up.

When I get back, Jake is still sitting in the chair. I grab my clothes and pull them on.

We still have an hour or so and I'd like to shower, but it's not like I can return back to work with wet hair so instead, we spend our time relaxing on the bed and he tells me about his trip, making me laugh with a story about the overly chatty guy he sat next to on the plane. I giggle and tease him and we just enjoy each other until the clock tells us that I need to get back to work.

I straighten the comforter on the bed and quickly wipe down the chair we used, grinning up at Jake. Then I wheel the cart out of the room, Jake kisses me goodbye, and I move on to the next room. I use my walkie-talkie to update my manager that the penthouse suite is clean. I can't keep the goofy grin off my face for the next hour.

CHAPTER TWENTY-FIVE

We settle into a little bit of a routine over the next week and a half. I run in the mornings, work, and then, most evenings, head over to Jake's condo directly afterward, where we eat dinner together, sharing about our day. It feels natural and comfortable and I've never been happier. I look forward with something very close to giddiness to greeting Jake at the end of the day. He picks me up and holds me close, kissing me, and spinning me around as if he hasn't been alive until that very moment.

But I'm also restless to know him better. I've been patient and understanding, but I want to know what he isn't telling me. I want to know the things that still clearly haunt him, that give him that faraway look when he thinks I'm not paying attention. There's something that separates us, and until he opens up to me, I fear I won't ever draw nearer to who he really is.

I'm also afraid that the reason he's not opening up is because he doesn't want to get closer to me, and this is his way of holding back.

A week later, on Friday night, we make love ardently, as always, and afterward, Jake wraps me in his arms, whispering intimate words to me as we drift off to sleep. But in the deep of night, I awaken alone and when I get up to seek him out, I find him standing silently on his balcony, drinking from a glass filled with amber liquid.

"Can't sleep?" I murmur, putting my arms around him from behind.

"Yeah." He sighs. "Thought a night cap would help. Go back to bed, baby, I'll join you in a minute." I notice his face looks strained.

"Okay," I agree, sleepily, squeezing him and then letting go, walking back to bed alone and a little troubled.

In the morning, he tells me he has a surprise. It's my day off and he's arranged a spa day for me. I'm excited because I've never, ever been to a spa before. I'm getting better at letting Jake treat me, even though it's still a struggle for me. He grins at my excitement and says it's all arranged. He scoots me into the shower and says a car will be here within the hour.

"Enjoy yourself, babe. I'm looking forward to meeting your friends tonight." It sounds nice, but he looks nervous and preoccupied and I don't know what to say to draw him out. Maybe he has a lot going on at work. I'll get the spa works today and then I'll do what I can to relax him tonight. I've become pretty adept at that.

"Why are you so good to me?" I ask, bringing my arms up around his neck.

"I love to spoil you. Making you happy makes me happy." He smiles, looking deeply into my eyes.

I shower quickly and then dress in dark gray yoga pants, a white tank, and light blue hoodie. I pull my sneakers on, and Jake and I eat a quick breakfast of cereal with fruit as I look over the brochure for the spa down the street.

I kiss Jake when the buzzer goes off in his condo and rush down to the waiting car.

I spend an amazing morning and afternoon at the luxurious spa a couple blocks down from his condo, getting the works: facial, manicure, pedicure, haircut and highlights, and a massage. I love everyone who works with me, and I spend the day not only relaxing and being treated, but chatting easily with the people who provide the services.

As I'm walking out of the massage room, getting ready to sign out at the front desk, a blonde coming down the hallway almost runs right into me. "Oh, excuse me!" I say, embarrassed.

"No problem," she mutters, stopping abruptly.

Oh my God, it's Gwen. *Holy shit!* Well, it *was* a nice day.

"Oh!" she says surprised, "Evie, right?" The look on her face tells me she's just about as happy to see me this time as she was the last, and the temperature in the spa seems to dip several degrees.

"Right. Hi, Gwen. Nice to see you." I try to make my way around her, but she sidesteps in front of me, blocking my escape.

"Funny running into you here. I'm assuming Jake sent you?" she says as if she knows very well I could never afford to come here on my own dime.

I pull myself up straight. If she's going to make a cat fight out of this, I'm not going to slink away like I have something to be ashamed of. "He did," I say, smiling a fake smile. "He likes to pamper me."

"Right," she says back, smirking. "I'll bet. Listen, Evie, I'm going to be a friend to you here and lay it on you straight. I know you probably think you don't have a lot of reason to trust me considering the last time we met I . . . exaggerated a couple things between Jake and me. But I feel like it might be in your best interest to realize a few things."

I stare at her, speechless, which I guess she takes as her cue to continue.

"I've known Jake a long time. In all states of . . . *sobriety*. He doesn't even know some of the things he's divulged to me when he was drunk or high off his ass. But, sober or not, it always comes down to the same thing. He'll never love anyone except *her*. If you think you love him, you should know he's just trying to turn you into her. I've seen him do it again and again. He takes a poor little mouse, uses her, gives her nice things, makes her think he has real feelings for her, and then throws her away when it becomes obvious that she's *not* her. You'll never be enough for him, Evie. It's not you he really wants."

At her words, I die a thousand deaths. It's my greatest fear. I'll never be enough for anyone. Not ever. No one ever wants to keep me. Not when it comes down to it. In my life, I've been thrown away again and again by those I thought loved me. I can't live through it again. I can't.

I push past her, trying desperately to get away from her words, cutting me to the bone.

"He has her picture on his back," she calls after me. "Surely you've seen it?"

I look back at her with wide eyes, mouth open in question and she just laughs. "He hasn't let you see. Typical. Run while you can, honey."

Then she turns and saunters down the hall while my heart shatters into a million pieces. I feel brittle, breakable, like I might crumble right there in the hall of the luxury spa. I walk to the counter—numb—and sign the paperwork. The girl behind the counter tells me that all costs, including tips, have been taken care of and that they look forward to seeing me again soon. I smile what feels like a broken smile and walk woodenly out the door.

Jake told me to text him when I was almost done and he'd send a car for me, but I don't call him. Instead, I walk the five or so blocks to his condo, my head swimming. I arrive at the front door, not even remembering the walk there. I ring the bell and the deskman opens it for me. His smile freezes on his face when he sees me, but he doesn't ask me what's wrong. He just buzzes Jake's condo and talks into the phone in quiet tones.

"Mr. Madsen will meet you outside the elevator," he says, guiding me inside and pressing in the code.

It takes a million years for the elevator to get to Jake's floor and when it opens, Jake is standing there, a perplexed look on his face. He takes one look at me and pales. "Evie, baby, what's wrong?" he asks as he puts his arms around me and leads me into his condo. I let him, not knowing what to do.

He closes the door behind us, and he turns me toward him, taking my face in his hands and looking in my eyes. "Evie, talk to me, love, what's wrong?"

"Take off your shirt, Jake," I say, my voice expressionless.

A look of confusion crosses his features. "What? Baby, I don't understand."

"Let me see your back, Jake," I say, gazing into his eyes, begging him to laugh and tell me I'm being ridiculous.

Instead, a look of dawning crosses his expression and he closes his eyes. When he opens them, he looks pained. "Evie, who did you talk to? Baby, let me explain first."

"No!" I scream, suddenly irate, voice shaking. "Show me your back, Jake!"

He closes his eyes again and drops his head, and then he looks me in the eyes as he reaches down and takes the hem of his shirt, lifting it up and over his head. For a second he just stands there, bare-chested, staring into my eyes, imploring me in some way I can't comprehend. Then, he slowly turns away from me, giving me his full naked back. He drops his head.

My eyes lift and I let out a gasp. For stretched across the entirety of the top half of his back is a tattoo, and as I study it, a strangled cry comes to my lips, and I stumble backward.

The artwork is done in shades of black, with beautiful scrolls around the edges. It's the inside of a circus arena. In the middle background is the master of ceremonies, his face turned sideways, lost in shadow. There's a little pale-haired girl walking a tightrope in the far right corner and several clowns, male and female, in the far right background. But when I look closely, their faces are not silly or funny, but ghastly, evil, sharp teeth dripping with blood, and eyes bloodshot and crazed.

And in the middle of the arena, the central art, there is a creature, half man and half lion with the man side facing slightly away so that his features are unclear and the lion side fully exposed, vicious and roaring, up on his hind paws, lunging toward a girl holding a fiery ring.

My eyes move slowly to the girl, as if in a trance, and my breath hitches in my throat. Her face is serene, calm, a slight smile on her lips, and she is looking directly at the man-lion, no fear in her expression at all. She is young, but I recognize her immediately. *She is me.*

And she is a lion tamer.

Oh my God. Oh God, oh God.

The moment slams into sharp focus, and I let out a quiet, strangled cry.

At the sound, Jake jolts, but he remains standing with his head hung, facing away from me. I walk around him and take his chin in my hand, lifting it so his tortured eyes meet mine. My hand is shaking, my heart is beating wildly, but I don't hear any expression in my voice as I look into his eyes and ask, "Why are you looking at me?"

His eyes search mine for several long seconds before he holds contact and whispers, "Because I like your face."

I stumble backward, crying out, and then turn and run. I fling his front door open and run to the elevator, pushing the button desperately. The elevator opens immediately. It never left his floor. I fling myself inside and push the lobby button. As the doors close, Jake appears in his doorway, a look of desperation on his face. "Evie," he chokes out just as the doors close.

I stumble out the front door of his building and I run.

CHAPTER TWENTY-SIX

I run until my lungs are burning and the tears running down my face have stopped falling. And then I walk, but I don't stop moving.

My mind is a jumbled mess and all I keep coming back to is that tattoo. At first I want to sob and scream, I want to beat my hands against something, but strangely, the farther I move from Jake, the more numb I become until I'm lethargically walking down the street. The tears are gone.

I stop when I see a small park and wander over to a bench. I sit down and pull my cell phone out of my purse. There are seventeen missed calls from Jake. I erase them and dial Nicole.

"Hey, babe," she says cheerily.

"Nicole," I start, but my voice breaks.

"Evie, what's wrong, honey?" she asks, concern spilling from her voice.

"He's been lying to me, Nicole."

"Who? Jake? Honey, about what? Where are you?"

"I ran. I don't know. I'm in a park . . . I don't know. Hold on, there's a sign . . ." I read her the name of the park and she says quickly, "I'll be there in fifteen minutes. Hold tight, honey."

I sit on the bench, staring into space until Nicole's small car pulls up next to the curb. I climb in, and when she sees my face, she opens her arms and I do a head plant into her shoulder. She holds me as I cry more tears I didn't think I had.

"What's going on, hon? Tell me," she says, wiping wetness off my cheeks with her thumbs.

"He's Leo, Nic. That story he told me about Leo dying in a car accident isn't true. Because *he's* Leo." I frown. "But he's Jake, too. I don't understand it."

Nicole looks stunned. "He's Leo? *Your* Leo? *The* Leo? But why didn't he tell you? How did you find out?"

"Nicole, can we go to your house? I want to wash my face and . . . is that okay?"

"Of course, let's go." She pulls out, and I lay my head back on the seat and close my eyes. Nicole must know I need to rest for a few minutes because she doesn't ask me any more questions on the drive.

We go into her house and it's quiet. "Where's Kaylee?" I ask.

"She's with Mike's mom today and tonight. I thought it might be nice to have an adult night since we were going to meet Jake." She shoots me a look and bites her lip.

I sigh. "Can I clean myself up a little bit? I'm a freakin' mess."

"Yeah, go do that and I'll make some tea . . . or do you want something stronger?" She smiles.

I laugh for the first time since I left the spa. "Later. For now tea is good."

I clean myself up in the bathroom, smoothing my hair back down which is all blown to heck, and holding a cold, wet washcloth on my eyes for a few minutes each. When I come out, I feel better.

I find Nicole curled up on one side of her sofa with a steaming cup of tea in her hand. She gestures to mine on the table next to the big, upholstered chair to her right.

I curl up and pull the afghan draped across the arm over my lap. I pick up my tea and take a sip as Nicole says, "Tell me what happened today."

I recount my run in with Gwen at the spa, and then when I tell her about confronting Jake and about his tattoo, Nicole sucks in breath and says, "What? YOU are the girl on his back? Okay, wow, this is blowing my mind. But wait, I don't get it . . . what does it mean?"

Haltingly, I tell her about Leo's family, his brother, his pain, and the story I'd made up to try to ease his suffering, at least momentarily. I only cry once during the telling of it, remembering a roof on a hot summer night and a broken boy in my arms.

I look up at Nicole and her eyes are glistening with tears, too. "Wow, Evie," she chokes. "He carried that with him on his skin all these years. That's just . . . wow. That's beautiful."

"He lied to me, Nic, *twice*. In my life, that *boy* destroyed me . . . and now the *man* has been deceiving me." I have no idea how to feel right now. My mind is reeling with hurt and confusion.

"Are you going to give him a chance to explain things to you, honey? I'm not saying you'll be able to forgive him. I have no idea what he'll say, but I think you need to listen to him." She looks at me worriedly.

I mull over her words for a few minutes and then I sigh. "I guess I owe that to myself, too. I just can't process all of this right now. I need time."

"Okay, hon. You go to him when you're ready. Just hear him out. You deserve answers."

I nod, taking a sip of my tea.

Nicole speaks again, haltingly, softly, "Honey, you really didn't recognize him? Not even a little bit?"

I'm silent for several minutes, sipping my tea, deep in thought about her question. "I mean, Nicole, he looks so different. I guess now that I know, I can see the boy that he once was in some of his features, but, I mean . . . okay, who was the first boy you kissed?"

Nicole grins. "Jimmy Valente. We were fourteen. He was my boyfriend for a year."

"Okay, can you conjure up his face in your mind right now?"

She looks up, concentrating, then frowns. "No, I guess I can't."

"Okay, well imagine that Jimmy Valente was a scrappy, skinny kid in worn clothes the last time you saw him, and then eight years later you came upon this huge, stunning, godlike creature in a designer suit, whose hair had darkened, who had gotten dental work done, and he told you his name was Tom Smith. You might not recognize him either."

I feel defensive, because truthfully, why *didn't* I recognize him? He was the love of my life, up until I met Jake anyway, or . . . wait . . . *God, this is all so messed up.*

"Also, Nic, you have to realize that after Leo left and didn't contact me again, it was so painful for me that, in my mind, he was still that boy on the roof with me, almost . . . I don't know, frozen in time. It was easier for me to convince myself that he remained there in a real sense. To picture him walking around in the world, not caring about me, hurt too much. I guess I compartmentalized him. There was the real world, and then there was that boy . . . lost in the past. Jake showed up and he was part of the real world, completely separate from that boy on the roof." I rub my eyes. "God, am I even making sense?"

"Yeah, I think I understand. I have some things in my past, granted, nothing overly traumatic, but you know, just things I prefer to *leave* in my past for one reason or another, and I put those things in a special category called 'things I've decided never to think about again'." She laughs a quiet laugh.

I smile. "Yeah, something like that."

We're both quiet again for a minute or two and then I say, "The thing is, I think a part of me did recognize him, something visceral, something more instinctual. I just didn't question it enough, because truthfully, I didn't want to. Maybe I did know and chose not to admit it to myself. I've always been good at shutting things out that felt unpleasant to me," I say sadly.

"Everything was just so intense with Jake . . . Leo . . . whatever. Jeez, this is like one of those crazy soaps where people are suddenly coming back to life all over the place."

I rub my sore eyes and Nicole looks at me sadly. "It came in handy for you for a long time. It was a coping mechanism."

I nod. We're quiet for a minute and Nicole is furrowing her brow. "What was Leo's full name?"

I reach back into my mind for a minute. Obviously I know his first and last name, but do I remember his middle name? And then my eyes widen and I whisper, "Leo Jacob McKenna." I drop my head to my hand. "Am I completely blind?"

"No," Nicole shakes her head, "everything seems clear now you know the truth. You were . . . caught up. It's not difficult to understand. But he owes you an explanation. He needs to tell you what the *fuck* happened eight years ago and why he's been lying to you about who he is now. Then you decide if you can accept what he has to say."

I feel the weight of the situation again and tears spring to my eyes. "I'm gonna lose him again, aren't I? Either that or I'm gonna have to let him go. I don't know if I can do it twice. I don't know if I'll survive it again." Pain grips me and I bring my hand up to my chest.

"Okay, don't panic. Let's just take this one step at a time. Mike will be home at five. We'll have a nice dinner, just the three of us. We'll have wine. You'll stay here with us tonight. You'll feel better in the morning, and then you can decide when you're ready to let lion boy have his say." She winks at me.

God, I'm so lucky to have her. Friends are the family you get to choose for yourself. It's never been clearer to me that I've made very good decisions in this category.

After dinner and catching Mike up on the twilight zone that is my life right now, we crack open a bottle of wine, and I actually giggle a time or two at their attempts to make me laugh with stories of their adolescent love failures.

As much as Mike and Nicole have been successful in distracting me, I know I'm going to have to face reality in the morning, so I borrow a pair of Nicole's PJs and turn in.

I climb into bed and turn on my phone. There are fourteen new calls from Jake/Leo. There are four text messages basically begging me to call him, and one voicemail. With shaking fingers, I listen to it.

I close my eyes as his voice comes over my phone. "Evie, God, I . . . please call me. I'm going crazy here. You ran and I don't even know if you're okay. Baby, please just let me know you're okay. At least that. Even if you don't want to talk to me . . . or, even if you don't want anything to do with me . . ." He pauses and I hear him take a shaky-sounding breath. "Please just let me know you're safe. I went by your apartment and you weren't there and it's late and I . . . please be okay." There's another pause before he clicks off.

A tear rolls down my cheek. What am I going to do? I type in a quick, two word text message to Jake/Leo: **I'm safe.**

I wait for a couple minutes, but there's no response. I turn off my phone again and fall into a fitful sleep.

****

The next morning I wake early and Nicole and Mike's house is quiet. Not wanting to wake them, I write a quick note and sneak out the front door quietly. I catch the bus to my apartment and let myself in. I linger under the hot water and when I emerge, I feel refreshed and ready to face the day, whatever it may bring. I dress in a pair of favorite jeans and a demi-sleeved, cowl-necked green sweater. I pull on my short brown boots and pull my hair back into a messy bun after I've partially dried it and put on some light makeup. I go through my routine in a daze, my eyes still slightly red and just a little bit puffy.

It's been weeks since I've done a proper shopping trip and so I leave my apartment in search of coffee. I walk to a Starbucks about twenty minutes away and forty-five minutes later, I'm caffeinated and have even eaten half a blueberry muffin, and feel semi-human.

I turn the corner to my apartment and immediately, I spy Jake's dark silver BMW parked out front. I walk slowly down the block, and he's in front of me before I even make it halfway there.

He looks like hell, like he hasn't slept a wink, and I can't help it, I want to soothe him. He has his hands in his jeans pockets, and he's looking at me, a look of longing and uncertainty, his gorgeous face a mix of insecurity that hits me right in the gut. That look, I realize—the one that made my heart beat faster in my chest right from the beginning—it's all Leo, my uncertain boy.

I know he's lied to me, and I know I should distrust him right now, but I can't help it, my heart is screaming at me, *your Leo is back! He's right in front of you! Go to him. Your beautiful boy is here. HERE!*

And the love that engulfs my heart is so overwhelming that I almost fall to my knees right then and there.

This is not good.

I want to be standoffish. I want to play cool, calm, and collected. I want to remain detached until he explains something to me that will melt my heart. I want there to be nothing he can say that will melt my heart. I'm pleading for him to say something that will melt my heart. I'm a mess.

And so I run. *Again.* I try to dash around him. I try to run fast and hard to the safety of my apartment. I try to escape my confusion and my fear, and yes, the love, but Jake steps to the side easily and scoops me up from behind. I fight him, but he's too strong, and he carries me to the door of my building, and he growls in my ear, "Give me your key, Evie," and like an obedient child, I take the key out of my purse, and I hand it to him. He's my boy, but he's also my lion. And God help me, I love them both equally. Still, it doesn't mean I forgive him.

Where is Maurice when I'm actually being manhandled?

He opens my front door and then he carts me inside like I weigh no more than a sack of rice. He uses the same key ring to open my inner apartment door, and then he sets me down inside, closing it behind him.

We stare at each other, him breathing harshly and me glaring, for several seconds.

Finally, he drops his head and runs his fingers through his hair. *Oh, God don't do that!* "Evie, we need to talk and we need to talk now."

"Why do you get to decide when we need to talk? Isn't it my call, *Jake*? Or should I call you Leo? Do you go by both? Please, clue me in here."

He closes his eyes for a minute like he's really just too tired to deal with my attitude. And isn't *that* priceless! "Evie. Please. Can we talk? Will you listen to me? This has been hell on me. Please. I just want you to tell me you'll *listen* to me—really listen to me."

"Hell on *you*? Oh, please, Jake. I don't want to make things harder on *you*. Please, sit down. Can I get you a beverage? A foot rub?" I glare at him.

He sighs as if he's barely tolerating me. "Sit down, Evie. Now."

I want to rail at him. I want to tell him to suck it. But, instead, I do as he says, sinking down on my couch while he continues to stand above me.

Finally, he exhales and runs his hand through his hair. *Again! How many is that now? He's trying to kill me.* He drops down on the couch with me, but at the other side.

"If you need something, go get it now. We're going to talk and this could take a while. Get what you need to make yourself comfortable, and then plant yourself on the couch."

I stare at him for several seconds and then exhale as well. "I'm fine, Jake . . . Leo. Please, let's get this over with." I pinch the bridge of my nose, massaging away a headache that hasn't even started yet.

He moves closer to me now and suddenly it's all just too much for me. The smell of him, the look on his face, my emotions, and I bring my hands to my face and I sob. Jake/Leo doesn't say a word, but I hear him moving closer, and suddenly I'm on his lap, being cradled in his arms, and his face is buried in my hair.

My hands come away from my face and I choke out, "I *waited* for you! I waited and waited and you just disappeared. I didn't know if you were dead or alive. I didn't know if you had just decided to start a new life and written me off, or *what*! And still I waited. And truthfully, even though I didn't even admit it to myself, I was *still* waiting until the day you walked back into my life, calling yourself by another name. I never stopped waiting for a boy who threw me away like I was nothing!"

I'm sobbing and choking and practically hyperventilating now, but

Jake/Leo just pulls me tight against his big body and rocks me, whispering sounds of comfort against my hair.

And how is it that this man can comfort me for any of this? He's the *cause* of these tears. And yet, I cling to him anyway.

After a few minutes, my sobs subside and I turn my face up to his. There are silent tears running down his cheeks as well. I take my thumbs and I wipe them off. Then my hands are on his face, my thumbs sweeping across his brow, his strong jaw, his cheekbones, down his nose, my eyes sweeping along with my fingers, taking in every part of his manly face, but finally seeing the boy that was there once, too, *letting* myself see the boy that maybe I knew was there all along.

My hands still and I gaze into his deep brown eyes, and then suddenly, somehow, we're kissing. His tongue is in my mouth and we're moaning, and when he drags my sweater over my head and pulls my bra down and teases my nipples with licks of his tongue, I gasp out his name, "Leo!" A deep, satisfied growl comes from his throat, and suddenly I'm on my back and he's over me, demanding, "Say it again."

"Leo, Leo, Leo," I moan out, reaching for him and wrapping my legs around him. "Make love to me, Leo."

I don't know what he's going to tell me about why he broke his promise to me, why he's been lying to me. I don't know whether I'm going to be able to forgive him or not. But, whatever happens, I want this. I want him, *my Leo*, with me crying out his name, *at least one time*.

He goes back to my breasts, pressing reverent kisses around my puckered nipples before suckling them one by one into his mouth. I'm writhing and rubbing myself against the hard erection I feel through his pants. I'm on fire, every nerve ending strumming with my desire for this man.

"Please," I beg. "I need you."

"My Evie," he breathes, leaning to the side, pulling my jeans and panties down, and dipping his hand between my thighs, moving his finger against my swollen nub, and returning his mouth to my breast.

He begins moving his finger in matching rhythm to the suction at my nipple and I bend one knee, letting it fall against the side of the couch, giving him more access.

I breathe his name, "Leo," as he replaces his finger with his thumb on my swollen bundle of nerves and slips one finger inside me and slowly moves it in and out, adding to the sweet pleasure. He's playing my body like an instrument and I'm drunk with arousal, heady with need. All rational thought is gone.

I open my eyes, my lids feeling heavy and I gasp out another moan. Leo has come up off my breast and is watching my face. His jaw is clenched with the effort to retain his control as he puts off his own pleasure to give me mine.

His fingers rub and thrust, constantly changing tempo, keeping me on the edge until I'm crazy with the need to come. "Leo!" I beg, my hips surging upward to claim my own satisfaction from his hand.

He adds another finger and picks up the pace, rubbing and thrusting rhythmically now. I moan loudly and breathe out, "*Yes.*"

Leo moans, too, and then the only sounds in the room are my panting breaths and the slick noises of his fingers pumping in and out of me.

"Come for me, Evie," he growls. And just like that, my body tenses and I arch up off the couch, intense waves of ecstasy flowing through me. I cry out his name and hear his zipper, and then he's flipping me over, and his hands are on my hips as he drags me up so that my ass is in the air, and he plunges into my dripping sex on one loud moan. I'm not sure if it's his or mine or both.

Up on his knees behind me, he begins thrusting his hips, moaning my name again and again, and I answer him, "Leo, Leo, Leo." My brain is cloudy with passion, but somewhere at the back of my mind, I understand that even though we have made love dozens of times, we're reuniting here and now as Evie and Leo, and I want to cry with the intensity of it.

He continues to thrust rhythmically, holding my hips steady so he can pound into me, and it's primal and almost rough, his cock hitting my cervix with every drive. I feel another orgasm building in my core as I listen to the rhythmic sound of his thighs slapping against my ass.

His breathing becomes labored as he continues to pant out my name, his thrusts becoming harder and faster, the scent of our combined sex filling the room.

He reaches around my hip and presses his finger to my clit, and I spiral straight into another climax, throwing my head back, and pushing my ass back to meet his thrusting cock. He growls and moans, and his strokes become slower as he glides in and out of me leisurely, drawing out his own orgasm.

He stops and lays his head against my back as our breathing slows.

We stay this way for long minutes, until my legs give out and I start sinking to the couch. He pulls out and catches me around the waist, turning me over. We cling to each other. He's leaned slightly to the side of me so I can take his weight. Finally as our breathing returns to normal, he sits up, pulling me with him, and placing me back on his lap again. He leans back against the couch and takes my face in his hands, looking deeply into my eyes. "I love you, Evie," he says quietly. "Whatever you think about what I'm about to tell you, you have to know that. I've always loved you. I've never stopped. Not for one second in eight years."

I nod at him, closing my eyes against the tears that threaten again. "Let me go clean up and then we'll talk, okay?"

He nods, pulling the zipper closed on his jeans and leaning forward on his thighs.

I pull on my sweater and jeans and go into the bathroom to clean up. When I get back, I sit on the couch next to Leo. He's still sitting with his elbows on his thighs, his head down, but as I sit, he leans back. He doesn't look at me for a minute and then, "I guess the best place to start is my arrival in San Diego."

CHAPTER TWENTY-SEVEN

"Okay, but first, why did you change your name?"

He sighs. "Lauren asked me if it would help me to get a new start if I began going by my middle name, and of course, my new last name. I said no at first, but after that first week, I agreed. I wanted to become someone else—truthfully, I wanted to escape myself. Of course, a name change can't do that, but it seemed like a start at the time. I registered for school as Jake Madsen and no one has called me Leo until now."

I nod. I can't pretend I don't understand this. At many times during my life, if someone had offered me the chance to become someone other than Evie Cruise, it would have been a very tempting offer.

"You have to know that when I left you here, I meant every word I said up on that roof that night. I meant it to my soul. I knew there would never be anyone else for me, and I was right. There never has been." He looks at me searchingly.

"You told me there were lots of women, Leo," I whisper, turning my head away from him to gaze out the window for a minute. I can't lie; it hurts deeply now that I know who he really is.

"None of them meant anything to me. Not one. Not even close. I'm not proud of that, in fact, I'm ashamed of it. But it was never anyone except you. I was fucked up, Evie. But I've never loved anyone except you. You have to believe that, even if you don't understand."

He sighs, dropping his head. When he looks back up, he says, "I arrived in San Diego on a Sunday night. On Monday morning, I started my letter to you. I wrote a little bit on Tuesday, and on Wednesday. I intended to write to you every day of the week until Friday, and then put the letter in the mail on Saturday. I stopped writing on Thursday."

"Why? What happened on Thursday," I ask quietly, looking back at him, but almost afraid to know.

He's silent for a minute and then, "On Thursday afternoon, I was down in the finished basement trying to learn how to play pool. We had this big pool table with red felt and . . . Anyway, I was just messing around. My new dad, Phil, was at work. My new mom, Lauren, as you know . . ." He pauses, grimacing a little. "She came down wearing this little nightie thing. I was uncomfortable, but I had never really had any kind of normal home life. I thought maybe that was what moms did. Walk around in their bedclothes. Or at least that's what I tried to tell myself."

My eyes are wide now because I'm pretty sure I know what's coming, and I don't know if I want to hear him say the words.

"She poured herself a drink and then she poured me one, too, and I took it, even though all kinds of warning bells were going off. I just didn't know what to do.

"We played pool for a little bit, and I finished my first drink and she poured me another. She was making all these shots, bending over the pool table and it was weird, but the alcohol started numbing me and so it was easier to pretend it was normal." He lets out a humorless laugh and then looks down.

He sighs and he's still looking away from me, but continues his story. "After a little while, she started rubbing up against me, touching me. I was a young, horny kid with two drinks in me, and I was confused and struggling with what was happening with this woman who I thought had taken me into her home to mother me."

He sighs again, looking tortured and deeply ashamed. "Shit, this is hard."

I want to touch him in some way, but I instinctively know that's not the right thing to do, so I remain silent and still.

After a minute, he continues. "Finally she just got completely naked and bent over the pool table and started begging me to take her. She seduced me, but I didn't resist very fervently. I fucked my new *mom* over the pool table in the basement while my new *dad* was at work. How fucking sick is that?" He lets out a harsh exhale and closes his eyes tightly for a brief moment.

Tears are rolling freely down my cheeks now and I choke back a little sob.

He continues staring ahead when he says, "We ate dinner that night as a family and my dad toasted to their 'new son.' I could barely keep the food down. I fucking hated myself and all I could think about was how I had done it once again. I had let someone down who loved and trusted me. *Again*."

He pauses for several minutes. "They had tried for several years, but never could have kids. Phil made it clear to me that he was thrilled to have a son now who could one day take over his company. We had talked a lot before that day, and he made me feel good about myself, like he thought I was smart."

When he pauses again, I manage to ask, "I thought you told me your adoptive father worked in a hospital here."

"He did. The X-ray technology that's now used by Homeland Security, started out as medical equipment."

I nod. "Sorry, go on, Leo," I say quietly.

A look of pain crosses his face when he hears me say his name, but he continues.

"Anyway, that afternoon in the basement was all it took to make me realize that once again, people only wanted to use me. First, my birth parents to take care of my brother and to take out their anger at the world on, and now these two people. My new mom for obvious reasons, but then it was also easy to twist my new dad's interest in having a son just to use as a workhorse, someone to train and mold into what *he* wanted me to be.

"No one ever cared about who I *was*, just what I could do for them, except you, Evie, and my brother, Seth. And now I had destroyed both of you. I had promised Seth I would take care of him, and now he was rotting in some state run facility somewhere, and I had no idea where, and I had promised you I would save myself for you, be true to you, and it only took less than a week for me to betray you. I honestly thought about slitting my own wrists I hated myself so much."

I grab a tissue from the box on the table next to my couch and blot my cheeks. "Leo, surely you know now that she took advantage of you, right?" I say quietly.

His face gets hard. "I know what all the psychology books would say about it and yeah, she was wrong. But I could have resisted more. I could have run. I could have . . . I don't know. But I could have done more than I did. And not only that, Evie, but it didn't stop that day. It happened regularly until the day I moved out and went to college. Even then, she tried to continue things, but I could successfully avoid her then. She claims she's in love with me and that she knew it the minute she saw me at the foster home. How twisted is that? Jesus. I was fifteen." He scrubs his hand down his face.

I cringe. "You didn't think you could trust me enough to tell me?" I ask softly, a sob making my voice hitch.

"A million times I thought about how I could explain to you what happened. I needed you so desperately. I thought I would die of the longing. But what was I supposed to say? I couldn't even make sense of it myself, much less try to explain it to you. I was just so deeply ashamed.

"And eventually, I considered the longing for you my penance for being *me*, someone who destroyed the people he loved. The thing I couldn't get around was what my silence must be doing to you."

He stares straight ahead, stoic. "Eventually, though, I convinced myself that being apart, you had a fighting chance. I figured I was broken and that some people can't be fixed, or if they can, it's only by love so big it destroys the fixer. I couldn't destroy you any more than I thought I already had, Evie. I convinced myself that knowing the truth about me would have hurt you more than leaving you alone.

"I just wanted to disappear. But you also have to understand that I hated myself for leaving. And I suffered as much as you did."

We're both quiet for several minutes, me still blotting my eyes, absorbing his answer, when he continues.

"I grew six inches the summer I moved to California, and I started playing sports, working out. It helped a little as an outlet, and I continued through high school, but it didn't help enough.

"I started drinking, doing drugs, partying, using girls. In part it was because I despised myself, and I craved anything that would numb my pain, but in part it was because it made Lauren livid to see me go through one girl after another, and I had grown to despise her, too. She's a manipulative bitch. She was lying to Phil, she . . ."

I interrupt him. "She's a pedophile, Leo."

He looks at me finally and says, "I guess, but I take responsibility, too. Especially, since it continued and it became our secret from everyone, especially my dad." He looks away, a look of shame crossing his face.

"Did you ever try to tell him?" I ask.

"A couple months after it started, I thought about telling Phil, but I felt so damn guilty and shameful for my own part in the situation. What if he didn't believe me? And what if he did and I destroyed them? Could I live with that, too? Eventually, I just focused on numbing myself.

"And then, even more shameful for me, I wanted to have a family so much. I loved all the things they were giving me; the luxuries, the trips, stuff I never had before. And that made me hate myself the most." He scrubs his hands down his face.

"Anyway, I was a fucking mess in high school. I dragged my parents through hell. Lauren always bailed my ass out with my dad, for obvious reasons, and my poor dad just tried to help me. But there was no help for me, not then. He had to think, *'what the fuck did we do adopting this kid?'* a million times, but he never, ever said that to me."

He rakes his hand through his hair. "Things started getting better for me when I moved out to go to college. I finally got some distance from my *mom*," he lets out a humorless laugh, "and started thinking a little more clearly. My dad and I were hanging out more outside of the house, and I developed a relationship with him—finally. He had to have been doubtful that I'd *ever* be trustworthy enough to learn the ropes at his company, but about a year after I was out of the house, he came to me and asked me if I'd work with him. I said yes and we started getting even closer. It was nice. He was a good guy, a workaholic and distracted, but decent and good.

"Anyway, when I graduated, he and Lauren bought me a Porsche as a gift. The night of my graduation party, Lauren cornered me in my bedroom and made another one of her passes. I pushed her off me, and she was pissed about it so she lashed out and told me that she hadn't wanted to break it to me this way, but that she had gotten information on my brother years ago from the family attorney." Pain moves over his face, but I don't reach out to him. I can't. I'm in information overload, and all I can do is take in what he's telling me and try my best to process it. All these years, all the heartache, all the grief and wondering, and now I finally know what happened. After a short pause, Leo goes on, "I was constantly asking Lauren to find any information she could so that I could visit Seth. She told me he died three years before of pneumonia, but she hadn't told me because she knew it would upset me. Jesus. Upset me? I practically raised that kid from the time he was born. And she just threw it out there because she was mad that I didn't want to have sex with her."

He stops and I can't help it, I grab his hand and I squeeze it. He turns his head to me. An expression of pain crosses his features again before he goes on.

"I tore out of there, taking my new car, driving like an idiot, tearing around corners, accelerating to speeds I knew were dangerous, suicidal even. I lost control, side swiped a semi and flipped my car six times. Or so I'm told. I don't remember any of it. The next thing I remember is waking up in the hospital with a head wrapped in bandages and tubes sticking out of me."

I suck in a breath.

"I had a fractured jaw, had shattered my right cheekbone and broken my nose all to hell, I had an eight inch gash across the back of my head, three cracked ribs, a ruptured spleen, two broken arms, and a broken leg. I was in the hospital for six months while they rebuilt my face and my body healed."

"Oh my God," I breathe.

He nods blankly. "I had nothing to do but lie there and self-reflect, so in one sense it was the best thing that could have happened to me. A part of me actually *had* died and was being reborn. I almost had no choice but to face my demons. The unfortunate part was that Lauren came to see me every day and there was nowhere I could run. One day after I had been there about a month, she came by to tell me that she had convinced them to let me come home with her after my next couple surgeries so that she could nurse me back to health. I protested, got angry, told her I was over eighteen and there was no way I was letting her get near me. She tried to convince me by throwing back the covers and going down on me." He makes a disgusted sound in the back of his throat and I wince. "There was nothing I could do. I was literally helpless to stop her, although I was railing at her to cut the shit, that I wasn't going to stay quiet anymore. That's when my dad walked in. She jumped back and we all just froze, stunned for several minutes, and finally he said, 'This is why? All these years, this is why you hated us both.' It was like it all finally just clicked into place for him. Then he started clutching his chest, and Lauren screamed and pressed the button for the nurse. He had had a major heart attack."

"Oh God, Leo," I whisper, more tears coursing down my cheeks.

He continues, but he sounds tired, almost monotone now. "He regained consciousness the next morning, and we thought he was recovering, but he got a blood clot five days later and that's what killed him. It can be common after a heart attack. The morning that he came to, they wheeled me in to him, and he put his hand over his heart and told me how sorry he was, and that he didn't blame me. I cried like a damn baby."

I squeeze his hand again.

"The day after that, his lawyers came to the hospital and he changed his will to give me full ownership of the company. Lauren has all she needs to live the life she's become accustomed to until the day she dies. But the company is a hundred percent mine."

We're both quiet for a minute as I consider something. "Was it Lauren who came to your hotel room in San Diego and answered your phone?" I ask quietly.

He runs his hand down his face again. "Yeah. She found out I was in town and surprised me in my room. I basically told her to leave or I'd call security. I know from experience how ugly it could have gotten, and I wasn't up for it, and so I told her that I was going to get in the shower, and lock the door and if she wasn't gone by the time I got out, I'd have her thrown out. I wasn't ready to give you details about her at that point and so I lied. It just felt like the lies were piling up, and I didn't know how to deal with it without telling you everything. What a fucking mess. And it was all my fault."

He pauses for a second and then continues. "She also came to the club we went out to that night with Landon and his friend. Joe, the lobby deskman told her where we were when she told him who she was. He won't make that mistake again. That's the point when I decided I needed to come clean with you. I just needed to figure out how to do it."

He takes a deep breath, seeming to rally a little bit. "Anyway, after my dad died, they sent the hospital psychologist up to see me the next day and I liked him, a real straight shooter, we hit it off. He started to come see me regularly after that and I opened up to him, the first time I had ever talked about my past, the first time I had talked about you.

"One of the things he said to me that really hit home was, 'Looking at the past can be painful, but you can either run from it, numb it, or learn from it.' I had run from it and I had numbed it. Neither one had worked. It was time for me to learn from it."

I close my eyes for a minute, and when I open them, we're both staring at each other with tears in our eyes.

"I realized that I couldn't remember a time when you weren't the first thing I thought of in the morning or the last before I fell asleep at night. You own me, Evie. You always have."

He shakes his head sadly. "It took almost dying to realize I needed to do something about that, fuck my fears. I couldn't deny you anymore. I was terrified, though, and I didn't know how you'd react to me. They had had to rebuild several parts of my face, nothing so drastic that I don't recognize myself, but enough so that, along with the other things that had changed about me since I was fifteen, I wondered if you'd recognize me right away.

"First time Gwen saw me when I moved here, she said she loved what the doctor had done to me, 'perfected me' she said. As if I had almost killed myself so that I could get some free plastic surgery. She's a piece of work."

We both actually manage a small smile.

"Do you have a picture of yourself before the accident?" I ask softly.

He thinks for a minute. "I have my old license. Hold on. He pulls his wallet out of his jacket and pulls it out and hands it to me. I see what he means. His face before the accident was still devastatingly handsome, but almost more rugged, less Hollywood perfect. Truthfully, he doesn't look *that* different, but I think I can see a little more of the boy that he was in it. I wonder, though, if that's just because I know who he is now.

He continues talking as I hand him back the card. "I took over my father's company when I got out of the hospital and told the board I'd be relocating to Cincinnati. And when I got here, I found you. I was so fucking nervous though. I had all these feelings wrapped up in you, and I had dreamed about you every night of the past eight years, but I didn't know if you were married, maybe had a kid . . . I didn't know. I also questioned whether you were the same girl I knew, whether my fantasies of you were partially of my own creation or if they were reality. So I decided to follow you around a little, get a feel for you. I realized that you were my same Evie, only, unbelievably, even more beautiful in every way than I remembered you. You took my breath away and I hadn't even gotten near you yet. I had thought about presenting myself as someone who had known Leo, but I wasn't sure the best way to play it or if you'd recognize me or what. I was trying to figure it out, trying to look at it from all angles when you surprised me. I know that sounds like I was trying to manipulate you, but you have to understand. I realized that I was even more deeply in love with you than I had been when I was fifteen and that was only from following you around for a week. I couldn't risk telling you the truth and having you run.

"You took me by surprise that day and forced me to make a decision on the fly. But when I realized that you didn't recognize me, I blurted out the lie about Leo dying. You told me that *he* had betrayed you, and so I just kept going with it. I just wanted to be near you so much. I didn't want you to tell me to leave you alone." He shakes his head, his expression filled with vulnerability. I look away, not ready to respond to that.

"I almost told you so many times. I was almost sure you realized who I was the night I drove you home from our first date and we sat in the car forehead to forehead, just exactly like that night I first kissed you on our roof."

I think back to that moment in his car, realizing I *had* felt something, but I had chosen not to examine it too closely. I had wanted so much just to bask in the new excitement of spending time with Jake.

I also think back to the strange moments in the penthouse suite at the Hilton when he surprised me. I had known then, too, hadn't I? Or in the nightclub when his angry expression as he protected me was somehow so familiar . . . But again, I had chosen not to think about what those moments meant.

Or how I had let him lead me so far out of my safety zone again and again, and how I had trusted him despite the questions that kept popping up and the things he wasn't explaining. Something in me had innately trusted him and now I understand why.

"I don't know if I did the right thing, Evie, but after I lied to you, I told myself that I'd just give it the time it took to make you realize that we belong together, and then I'd tell you the truth. It just got harder and harder to do and I was so damn happy to have you back in my life, to get to hold you, and make you smile, and also to re-discover you, that I kept putting off the moment when you might decide to leave, the moment when you might tell me you couldn't forgive me for abandoning you."

He runs his fingers through his hair and pauses before continuing.

"I'm so sorry. I'm sorry for hurting you, for lying to you, for all the lies that kept piling up, but I can't completely regret what I did, because it made you realize what we are together, without having to address the way I hurt you eight years ago right away, without having that baggage. I knew we'd have to go there eventually, but I can't be sorry that you saw who we still are together, before having to face the hurdle of our past. Does that even make sense? Does that make me a complete asshole?"

I take a deep breath before answering him. "I don't know, Leo. What I do know, though, is that I can't even completely put all the responsibility on your shoulders. If I'm honest, all along I felt like something between us was so familiar, something was niggling at me the whole time, and I chose not to address it, even to myself."

I pause and he lets me gather my thoughts before I continue.

"I've always been good at pushing things aside that I didn't want to think about, good at losing myself in my own head. It's why I'm good at making up stories, I think. Being able to escape to a dreamland was a survival instinct for me. Maybe I did that with you, too. Inside I knew that there was something I wasn't allowing myself to think about. I *let* you lie to me because the lie felt good. I admit that now."

He turns to me fully, his eyes pleading. "I won't let you take responsibility for any of this. Maybe you made some unconscious choices, but you can't blame yourself for that. I made all the conscious decisions. I'm the only one at fault in this situation. I understand that you need space to digest it all. But please, please, Evie, I can't lose you again. I'll never survive it twice. Can you at least try to forgive me? To understand why?" His voice is choked.

I pause and then say quietly, "I don't know. I just need some time, Leo. You've just caught me up on eight years of life . . . a really fucked up life . . . for both of us." I laugh humorlessly. "Can we . . . can I have some space to think? Please?"

He stares straight ahead for a minute, and then he starts to stand, leaning his elbows on his knees and looking me in the eye. "Yeah, it's hard for me because we've lost so much time already. But yeah, I'll give you whatever you need."

He stands up and heads straight for my door. He puts his hand on the doorknob, but doesn't turn it, and doesn't turn to look at me as he says, "Your gift with storytelling, Evie? It's not about you getting lost in your own mind, or living in a dreamland. It's about the beauty of your heart. It's about being able to rise above even the worst of situations. It's one of the reasons I've loved you every single day since I was eleven years old."

And with that, he opens my door, exits, and closes it quietly behind him.

I stare at the closed door for a minute, and then I draw my knees up to my chest, close my eyes and let the tears fall once again.

CHAPTER TWENTY-EIGHT

I end up falling asleep on my couch, exhausted, mentally and physically by everything that's happened over the past twenty-four hours.

I feel achy and hollow, and I think, numbly that this must be what people mean when they say they're "heartsick."

When I wake up, it's after eight, and so I put a single-sized frozen pizza in the oven, and then stand at the kitchen counter, barely tasting the food I'm eating.

I fall into bed at ten after watching *Braveheart* on DVD, and I sleep straight through until seven in the morning when my alarm goes off.

I drag myself to work, and as I pull my cart into the penthouse suite, memories of Jake and me, no *Leo*, in the chair in the bedroom assault me.

I put in my headphones and begin to clean, and my mind goes to work, too, trying to make sense of everything Leo dumped in my lap yesterday.

I'm not, by any means, an expert on male sexual abuse, but I have to imagine that it's a really complicated issue, since the abuser most likely doesn't use force or violence. Lauren definitely didn't, although it's clear to me she took advantage of the naiveté and innocence of a minor, her *son* for God's sake . . . Even if Leo himself refuses to put the responsibility entirely on her shoulders. And he *does* hold some responsibility of his own, doesn't he?

Maybe I should talk to an expert on this subject to try to

understand it better? God, what a completely disgusting situation. I thought I had heard it all. But it was always these types of stories that *preceded* kids getting put in foster care. I shake my head.

But what of his decision to let me hang because of his own shame? I think back to the devastation and desperation I felt as the months went by with no word from him. And then I picture him there in San Diego, numbing himself with alcohol and drugs, having sex with multitudes—apparently—of random girls and then women.

I cringe. But, *God*, he was fifteen! And he was a kid from a messed-up background, with absolutely no one to guide him. He made the wrong choice, but can I forgive him *now* for what he did *then*, knowing he'd go back and council that hurt, confused kid if he could and help him make a different decision?

And then the third issue, the lie he told to insert himself into my life, *again* putting his own needs and wants before mine. I can't completely say that his thinking was off base. As I'm pondering all this, I have the advantage (disadvantage?) of knowing that Leo and I are magic together, we fit in every way there is to fit. It would be easier to write Leo off as someone from my past who let me down and can't be trusted if I wasn't intimately acquainted now with the man. And he's a good man. I can't deny that.

Is this so confusing? Am I answering my own questions easily? Or am I trying too hard to make this okay because I'm in love with Jake, er, Leo Madsen?

I stop vacuuming as that thought resonates. I'm in love with Jake/Leo Madsen. Yes, I'm definitely in love with the man. I have been for a while now. I loved the boy, yes. I loved him deeply. But my love for the man is with an intensity I never could have imagined when I was fourteen years old.

I just need to live with these thoughts for a day or two. I'm sorry, Leo. I know you don't want to give me a lot of time, but you can't rush this either. I push my cart out of the room and continue down the hall.

****

The next day, I meet Landon for coffee after work and fill him in on everything that's happened since I last saw him, finally also telling him all about Leo . . . Jake . . . who is Leo. *God!*

He stares at me with his mouth hanging open slightly after I've talked for a solid thirty minutes.

"Is there a reason you invited me to *coffee* to lay all this on me, instead of meeting me in a bar for shots? Jesus!"

I smile softly. "Yeah, I'm on the wagon temporarily. If I start drinking now, I might never stop."

"Right. Well, wow is the understatement of the century. What are you going to do?"

I sigh. "I'm still trying to figure it out." Then I start telling him what I've worked out so far and why.

He nods. "I don't condone lying, Fancy, but if I think about it, I can understand his case for wanting to start out with a clean slate and see what you two could be all about together. I don't know that it was right, and it certainly wasn't honest, but I can see where his mind was."

I nod, biting the inside of my cheek. "I don't like it, but at the same time, it is more difficult for me to discount the fact that we are really good together. What's hard is that I think I would have given him a chance to explain, and I would have tried to listen to him if he had just presented himself as Leo right off the bat." I frown. "I think."

Landon nods, looking thoughtful. "He didn't want to count on that, though. And he had just spent six months lying in a hospital bed realizing that you were, *and are,* the only woman he'll ever love. He kind of had a lot riding on you accepting him back into your life." He holds his hands up. "Just playing devil's advocate."

I sigh. "I know. There are just so many different levels of emotion for me. I'm trying to sort through them all."

He's quiet for a minute or two. "You know, I know a little bit about male sexual abuse." He's looking at me nervously.

"What?" I whisper. "Oh my God, Lan, you never said anything."

"I know. It's a really hard topic for me even though I've made a lot of peace with what happened to me. I wanted to tell you so many times, but it's just such a hard thing to bring up. I have to give Leo props for talking about all the details of it with you. It's a really confusing issue for us survivors."

"Who was it? How old were you?" I ask quietly.

"I was fourteen. It was a neighbor who was a few years older than me. Thankfully, he moved away shortly after he started abusing me. But I carried it with me for a while before I finally told my mom. I had started acting out and she was confused, didn't understand why. One day I broke down and told her everything. She got me into counseling really quickly after that."

He goes on, "One of the most confusing parts for me was feeling like I must have wanted it to happen since my body cooperated. It sounds like maybe Leo struggles with that issue, too. It's pretty common."

I nod. "Definitely. He takes responsibility for letting it happen, and then letting it continue."

"The thing is, perpetrators of sexual abuse are master manipulators at making their victim feel at least partially responsible. That way, they're less likely to report it. Plus, he had the added element of his abuser being a woman and his adoptive *mom*."

He grimaces, but continues, "Talking to an expert would help him see that acting out and being sexually promiscuous is actually *really* common for people who have experienced something like he did. I don't know if I would be doing as well as I am without having talked to someone about it."

My eyes well up and I take Landon's hand. "Thank you for sharing your story with me. Just another reason why you're so incredible, Lan."

He smiles. "I know you have a lot of feelings wrapped up in your boy, good and bad, and I know that you're still deciding if you're going to be able to move past the things he is responsible for that hurt you. But he's a survivor, too, just like I am, and he deserves a lot of credit for coming out on the other side of that. Not everyone does so well."

I squeeze his hand and say, "Have I told you lately that I love you?"

He grins and winks at me. "I don't blame you. I'm very lovable."

****

I spend the next couple of days laying low. I basically go to work, come home and go back to work.

I spend two hours on the phone with Nicole Monday night updating her, and although re-telling Leo's story makes me emotional once again, Nicole succeeds in making me laugh as usual. I have such amazing friends.

When I get home from work Tuesday night, there's a manila envelope under the door of my apartment, and I open it up as I kick off my shoes, arching and flexing my feet to work the soreness out.

There are two pages inside and I pull out the first. My breath catches as I realize that it's from Leo and I realize what it is. It's the letter he had started writing to me when he arrived in San Diego.

Oh God!

I fall to my couch and with shaking hands, I start reading his teenage handwriting. *He kept it.*

Monday:

Dear Evie,

I miss you already. So much, you wouldn't even believe. Or hopefully you would, because hopefully you're missing me just as much.

We flew in over the ocean last night and all I could think of was how much I wanted to be having that experience with you. I keep collecting things in my mind that I want to tell you, show you, experience with you. I'm going to write them all down so that when I come for you in just four short years, we can start on the list. Nothing is as fun or interesting as it is with you. I don't know how you do that—how you make the most mundane things seem magical. Maybe that's just what love does. And I do love you, Evelyn Cruise. I love you down to my bones.

 P.S. I put my address and phone number at the bottom of this letter. Write to me as soon as you get this!

Tuesday:

 E—It's so weird to call someone else mom and dad, but that's what Lauren and Phil have asked me to call them. Phil seemed more enthusiastic about it and Lauren looked kind of mad, but I think it might just be because she thinks she looks too young to have a teenage son. She's pretty for a mom, but no one is as pretty as you. When you look at me with your big, brown eyes and you smile that smile reserved just for me, I think my heart is going to beat right out of my chest. I'm picturing your perfect lips right now and I want to kiss you again so much it hurts. I keep reliving our kiss and thinking about how it was the best moment of my whole life.

 My mom (Lauren) asked me today if I might want to start going by Jacob, or Jake, as sort of a fresh start here. I thought about it and I thought about how it might be nice to leave the person that I was in the past, to leave my life there behind. But then I realized that that would include you and so I said no.

 Yours, L

Wednesday:

Hi, Evie,

 We went to a restaurant last night where the ocean waves come right up on the glass windows! It was wild, but beautiful. I didn't want to tell my mom and dad that it was the first "real" restaurant I had ever been in because whenever I say stuff like that, they get these sad looks on their faces and it makes me feel small. I know you know exactly what I'm talking about. You always do. That's the thing I miss the most about being with you.

    I felt sad in the pit of my stomach when I thought about that last night and so instead I thought about how this was the place I was going to take you when I propose to you. I guess it won't be a real surprise if I tell you now, but you already know I'm going to marry you someday and so it's okay if you know the place I want to ask you. I'll try to keep the ring and the words I plan to say to you under wraps. haha.

I love you, Evie. I'll love you forever.

Your Leo

I sob, hot tears of sorrow coursing down my cheeks as I picture myself waiting for that letter and I picture Leo writing it, still hopeful, still my beautiful boy, up until that very next day.

I want to punch something, to throw something and hear it shatter, to make the sound that should accompany the feeling in my chest.

When I calm down, I sit staring at the wall for several minutes, gathering myself before I pull out the second letter, obviously written recently, in his adult hand.

To my Evie, the one who knew how to love me before I knew how to love myself,

I already told you about how I laid in that hospital bed for six months, reflecting on my life, reflecting on all the reasons that I couldn't stand to be alone with myself long enough to really think about who I was or what I was feeling.

What I didn't tell you was what a central role you played in helping me move toward a place of healing. My Evie, the strongest, purest person I've ever known. A person who was placed in the worst of circumstances in this life and yet selflessly loved and cared for those around her. How was it that someone so full of goodness and light ever even noticed a person like me? How did you see in me—what I was struggling so hard to see in myself?

I kept wondering why, all those years, when you looked straight into my eyes, unflinching, seeing the real me, what made you linger and come back? What made you love me despite who I believed myself to be? I thought about that hour after hour, and the only conclusion I could come to was that maybe, just maybe, there was something decent in me, maybe something that was close to good. It was the first time I had ever had that thought and it stunned me just to ponder the possibility.

All those months, staring at the ceiling and staring into my own soul, you, Evie, you were the miracle that I kept coming back to again and again—that all those years ago, you chose me.

Please, please, choose me again.

I will spend my life trying to make myself a person who is worthy of you. I will work until my dying day to give you the beautiful life a beautiful person like you deserves. I will prove to you that forever is not just a word, not just a measurement of unending time, but that forever is a place where I will treasure your heart.

Yours always, Leo

Tears streak down my cheeks as I clutch the two letters to my chest. I sit like that for long minutes, making a decision.

I take a quick shower and pull on jeans, a turquoise peasant top, and my brown boots.

I decide to call a cab. I finish putting on some makeup, partially dry my hair, and smooth it back into a low ponytail.

When the cab rings my cell phone, I run out and jump in quickly.

I look up the address of Leo's company and give that to the driver. I lean back as the city goes by, my heart beating peacefully in my chest. I feel sure and calm. I feel like all the pieces have fallen into place. I feel like this was always my path, and now I'm finally back on it.

I walk into the huge lobby of the mostly glass building. As I'm walking toward the deskman, I spot an all glass elevator starting its ascent. I see an unmistakable pair of broad shoulders among the group riding the elevator, but his back is to me. I rush toward it, looking up at it and catch the eye of a tall, dark-haired man who smiles at me. I start waving my hands and pointing at Leo, and the man finally understands, tapping him on the shoulder and gesturing out to me. He turns around as if in slow motion, and I will never, ever forget his expression, not until my dying day. He's confused at first, but as he sees me smiling up at him, I mouth, "I choose you," and understanding dawns, and a look of raw emotion like I've never seen fills his beautiful face.

He starts pushing through the people to the front of the elevator, and it stops suddenly at the next floor.

Then he's running toward the escalator nearest him, even though it's going in the wrong direction.

I run toward it as he starts parting the crowd, leaping down three and four stairs at a time to the yells and disgruntled sounds of the people trying to go upward.

He doesn't care though. His focus is singularly directed at me as he finally leaps over the railing close enough to the bottom not to hurt himself.

We rush into each other's arms, him spinning me around, his face pressed into my hair as I laugh and cry and continue to chant, "I choose you, I choose you, Leo. Always."

We suddenly realize that people are stopped around us clapping and whistling, and he grins at me, his face beaming with love and happiness.

"I love you, Evie," he says, his face sobering.

"I love you, Leo, my loyal lion."

"You still believe that, after everything?" His eyes are wide, looking deeply into mine.

I nod. "Even more. You found the courage to jump through fire for me. You found yourself on the other side, didn't you?"

He looks at me for long moments. "I guess I did. But you were the one holding the ring."

"That's the easy part, my beautiful boy. Believing in you is effortless. It always was."

He continues looking at me; that fire I love entering his deep brown eyes. Then he grins. "I'm going to take you back to my den and maul you now."

I grin back. "Yes, please."

And we walk out the door hand in hand, into our forever.

EPILOGUE

Seven Years Later

I stand on the balcony of our home watching my wife play in the pool below with our boys, Seth, six, and Cole, four.

As always, the sight of my wife in a bikini has my attention, first and foremost.

But then I laugh quietly as my youngest tries to dunk his older brother in a stealth attack.

I walk back into our bedroom, pulling on my swim trunks. I smile as I glance at the laptop open on Evie's writing desk. Her first book is almost done and maybe I'm biased, but I think it's brilliant. She says she doesn't care whether it's a hit or not, the success for her is in writing it at all, in stepping out of another safety zone.

The empty cup sitting to the side of her computer says, *World's Greatest Mom*. She bought it for herself.

I step out onto our patio and my boys shout, "Daddy!" in unison as I run and cannonball into the pool, drawing a shriek from Evie as my splash drenches her. She jumps in, too, wrapping her arms around my neck, and we're both laughing and kissing as our boys shout, "Ewww!" from the other side of the pool.

Our firstborn, Seth, is the spitting image of me and yet has the gentle, steady spirit of his mother. He is easy to smile and the first to lay a hand on your shoulder if you've had a rough day. He finds the beauty in everything.

We hadn't waited long to have him. We were young, but our forever was something that we were eager to begin. Time had taken enough from us.

The day in the hospital when he was handed to me, I looked into his eyes, still shaky and on an emotional high from watching my wife fearlessly bring him into the world, and I saw a depth there that didn't seem to belong to a newborn boy. He didn't cry, but gazed steadily at me as if he saw right into my heart. And his eyes seemed to tell me that, like his mother, he was satisfied with what he saw. I silently promised him that I would never take that for granted.

His brother, our Cole, looks just like Evie, with dark hair and large, dark eyes and a smile that lights up any room. He came screaming into the world and hasn't stopped making noise since. I smile. He is my rambunctious cub, always pouncing and laughing, full of energy and life—fiercely loyal and passionate. My wife tells me she sees me in him and I can only feel confused when she says it. But she always did see the best in me. Maybe he's who I would have been if I had been given the same start in life. More often than not, she has me convinced that there's something to her theory. Because that's who she is. It's her gift.

Everyone tells a story about who they are in their own head. That story defines you, dictating all your actions and all your mistakes. If your own story is filled with guilt and fear and self-hatred, life can look pretty miserable.

But, if you're very lucky, you might have a person who tells you a better story, one that takes up residence in your soul, speaking louder than the woeful tale of which you've convinced yourself. If you let it speak loudly within your heart, it becomes your passion and your purpose. And this is a good thing, the best of things. Because it is the very definition of love, nothing less.

Many years ago, Evie asked me about my tattoo, and I told her that I had gotten it on her eighteenth birthday, the day we were supposed to start our life together.

I had spent months designing it with a tattoo artist using the only photo I had of my Evie, one she had given me when she was thirteen. On that morning, I stepped into the shop and didn't step out until it was well after dark.

Then I had gone home and drank myself into a stupor, trying desperately to shut out the pain and the emptiness.

She traced every element of it silently, and finally her first question was why the master of ceremonies was cloaked in shadow. I had turned toward her and looked into her deep brown eyes and told her that it was because at the time, I hadn't known whether, he, the one who orchestrates it all, is kind or whether he is cruel.

Some days I'm still not completely sure. But other days, I look across at my wife's beautiful face gazing at me with eyes full of love, or I watch my sons wrestling together on our floor, filling our house with laughter, and I think that he must be kind.

All the world's a circus. Sometimes you choose your act and sometimes it's assigned to you. I had roamed the arena for far too long, roaring and bellowing, believing that I wasn't brave enough to leap through fire. But all along, she had stood there, constant and calm. "I can't make the fire go away," she had seemed to say. "I can't guarantee you won't get burned. But I can hold this hoop for you. I can remain steady and strong, because I believe in you. Because you are mine."

And in the end, I had jumped. And the other side was just as glorious as her eyes had promised.

Acknowledgments

A very special thank you to my girls - my beta readers, and my own personal cheering section! Your encouragement was invaluable to me. I never would have had the courage to hit publish without you. From Croatia to California, you rock the house down!

About the Author

Mia Sheridan is a *New York Times*, *USA Today*, and *Wall Street Journal* Bestselling author. Her passion is weaving true love stories about people destined to be together. Mia lives in Cincinnati, Ohio with her husband. They have four children here on earth and one in heaven. In addition to Leo, Leo's Chance, Stinger, Archer's Voice, Becoming Calder, Finding Eden, Kyland, Grayson's Vow, Midnight Lily, and Ramsay are also part of the Sign of Love collection.

Mia can be found online at www.MiaSheridan.com or www.facebook.com/miasheridanauthor.

Printed in Great Britain
by Amazon